REHNQUIST

GARY E. BOSWELL

ISBN-13: 978-1534772519

ISBN-10: 1534772510

DEDICATION

This book is dedicated to my loving wife Marcia, who has always believed in me and encouraged me to write this first novel. Thank you for your ideas, suggestions, proofreading, and multiple manuscript reads.

It is also dedicated to the memory of our son, Ian Merritt Boswell, in celebration of his short, well-lived life.

ACKNOWLEDGMENTS

I wish to express my appreciation to writer Marjorie K. Doughty, whose sage advice, "Write thirty minutes a day, and in a year you'll have a book," was sufficient to motivate me to stop procrastinating, and start writing. Thank you for the conversations, inspiration, and encouragement.

I'd also like to thank all my Sunday brunch buddies for their encouragement, and for tirelessly listening to me babel about writing week after week.

Chapter One

He pushed back his gin and tonic, reached for his cell phone and began looking at the day's emails. A half-dozen in, he became distracted at the sight of an attractive young server talking to a group of young men sitting at a high top near the end of the bar. She was standing in profile, long blonde hair and a rock-hard body, her skintight V-necked top taut over ample breasts. He wasn't paying attention earlier, but now she was hard not to notice. She was maybe nineteen or twenty, with a certain childlike innocence, and it was obvious that the customers at her table were interested in more than just dinner. As she turned in his direction and made her way to the POS terminal to enter their order, he caught a full frontal view of her face. Her innocence was, perhaps a bit too childlike, and he was ashamed that he had even noticed her. Now he felt like a pervert, an *old* pervert, or maybe just old.

He finished his gin, motioned for the bartender, and went back to his emails. A heavily cologned man half his age slid onto the barstool next to him. Eyeing the empty glass, he asked, "Can I buy you a drink?"

"No!" he snapped, leaning ever so slightly away from his new friend. Suddenly aware of his terse response, he looked up, turned to face him and said, "Sorry. Thank you . . . I'm waiting on someone."

Raising both arms as in surrender, the broad smile on the young man's face tightened slightly, and he said, "No problem," as he slid over one barstool to the right, as if to leave space for the expectant visitor.

No problem? The guy must work in retail or food service. We've lost an entire generation to poor manners, he thought. He hated it when he said 'thank you' at the register only to be answered by, 'No problem.' Of course it's no problem. What the hell happened to 'thank you,' or 'you're welcome?' *Besides, what kind of response is 'No problem' to a rejected pickup line?*

His gaze followed the young man to his new seat. *Shit. Twice in one week. Either one hell of a coincidence, or I'm sending out the wrong signals.* He didn't know whether to feel angry or flattered. He chose flattered, and went back to his email.

"Another?" the bartender asked.

Looking up, he briefly made eye contact and said,

"Vodka cranberry. Absolut please. Double. And light on the ice."

The barkeep's short hesitation was immediately met with an explanation, "I never drink the same thing twice." As he turned to make the drink, the bartender answered his explanation with a muted grunt and shrug.

Bored, he put down his phone and glanced up at the TV. ESPN. Basketball. Second only to tennis as the most boring sport in the world. He didn't know shit about it or the teams, and didn't care to. All he saw was a bunch of men running back and forth, their near-endless scampering occasionally interrupted by foul shots. Mind-numbing. Not at all like football, with its short, well-choreographed plays.

"Thank you," he said as the bartender set his drink down in front of him.

"It's what I live for," he replied, with no hint of a smile.

He picked up his vodka and took a sip, and then another, and soon became lost in thought, his mind drifting back to another time and place, many years before. A better time, when he still cared about life, and still cared about living. A time when something in his life really mattered, beyond just getting though each day. For a moment he found quiet solace in his escape, until the sound of a soft voice calling his name brought him back to reality.

"Mr. Rehnquist?"

For a half-second he was startled, then he turned and looked into the sad blue eyes of a blonde stranger. She was dressed in a white, short, sleeveless sundress with a dark purple hibiscus print, a small white purse slung over her left shoulder. White-framed Ray-Ban's rested atop her straight, shoulder length hair, and her lips were lined with a delicate pink lipstick. In the air stirred a fragrance that kindled a distant memory.

"Nick, please, and you must be Mrs. Roberts," he said, smiling as he rose to greet her. Standing, he immediately became aware of her height, as they stood nearly eye-to-eye. *Impressive for a woman*, he thought, as he was just under six, three. *All the more impressive, she's wearing sandals.*

"Grace," she replied, returning the smile as she extended her hand. "And, there's no missus, I dumped the mister years ago."

"You're early, Grace."

"So are you. Punctuality—I like that in a man."

"I like it even better in a woman."

"Thank you for agreeing to see me. Is there someplace we can talk a little more private?"

He pointed to an empty table at the far end of the small dining room.

"That's fine," she said.

Rehnquist spoke to the hostess and closed out his tab, and then he and Grace moved to the seclusion of the half lit dining room. Grace sat down at the table with her back to the wall, and Rehnquist sat down next to her. Motioning to the empty chair across from her, he said, "I hope you don't mind, I have this thing about sitting with my back to the door. Too many years as a cop I suppose."

"No, this is fine, and it makes it easier to talk."

"Good."

Robyn, the young server who had earlier caught Rehnquist's attention, brought them two menus, introduced herself, rattled off the day's specials, and offered to bring a round of drinks.

Grace said, "I'll have the house Chardonnay please."

"And you?" Robyn asked, turning to Rehnquist.

"I'll have a Martini, Grey Goose, dirty," he said with a wink.

Robyn nodded and walked off toward the bar, stopping on the way for a little more banter with the boys at the high top.

"What can I do for you, Grace?"

"It's my brother, Jason. He's missing, and I'm afraid that he's dead."

Chapter Two

"I'm sorry," Rehnquist said, raising his brow. "You're afraid that he's dead? Why? What makes you think that?"

"I haven't heard from him in two weeks. His phone goes straight to voicemail, he's not responding to texts, and emails sent to him are returned immediately, saying it's an invalid address. *And*, he hasn't been home."

"Please forgive the question, is it unusual not to hear—"

"Yes." she interrupted, "Jason always calls me—and usually Mom—everyday, even if only for a moment. Then one day, he suddenly stopped calling."

"And you contacted the police?"

"We did, and basically they just blew us off. They *looked into it*," she said, motioning with air quotes. "A week later they said that they could find no evidence of foul play, and that they could only assume that he just ran off and didn't want anyone to know where he was, or what he was up to—which is crap. Jason would never run off."

"Is it even a possibility?"

"No! Nick, I know my brother," she said in exasperation. "Like I said, Jason called me every day. Before this, I can't tell you the last time that we went over a day without talking—much less two weeks." Grace looked off toward the bar and sighed. How could she convince a perfect stranger of what she only knew in her heart, other than that there was no logical reason for Jason not to call. Everything was fine the last time they spoke, and even if it wasn't, and something had upset him, he still would have called.

Robyn returned, tray in hand, and sat a glass of ice water in front of each of them. She nodded to Rehnquist and then turned to Grace, "Have you been to Jake's before?" she asked.

Grace replied, "No—but you were recommended by a friend of mine who is nurse over at the hospital. She eats here occasionally after work, and said that the food is great."

"I think so," Robyn said, and smiled. "Have you had a chance to look at the menu? The specials are *really* good."

Grace stared blankly at the menu in front of her. She wasn't really hungry, but figured that she should have something. "Can I just get a Caesar salad?"

"Certainly," Robyn said, as she slid Grace's Chardonnay in front of her. Then she stepped around to Rehnquist and sat a frosty three-quarter full martini glass in front of him, and off to its left, its companion; a full sidecar, resting patiently in a glass of ice. "John said if it's not dirty enough, send it back, and he'll make it right."

Rehnquist held the martini up to the suspended table lamp, carefully inspecting the delicate, icy haze. "Perfect," he said, "thank you." Looking back at the menu, he said, "How about a burger, medium, with cheddar? Oh, and no bun."

"Fries?" Robyn asked.

"Sure, why not?"

"You got it," Robyn said. She collected the menus, and headed back toward the bar, with only a slight diversion past the high top to check on the boys.

"A burger," Grace said, with a frown, "and I took you for the healthy type."

"That *is* healthy. No bun, and the vodka keeps my cholesterol in check," he said, thumping his fist against his chest over his heart.

"If that's true, your cholesterol must be quite low," she said, smiling as she watched him savor the first of his drink. She was thankful for the brief moment of levity. It gave her a chance to collect her thoughts. "I'm impressed with the pour."

"Me too," he said. "It pays to tip well. Guess John and I are friends now. Actually, I tip well even when the service sucks. I worked in a restaurant once—as a kid. Two days. I screwed up every other order. I couldn't handle it, so I appreciate anyone who can."

"I do too," she said, reaching into her purse. She rummaged for a moment and then pulled out a faded, borderless color photograph with a small pinhole in the top center, and handed it to Rehnquist. Two teenagers were standing arm-in-arm on a long finger pier next to a flats boat. Off in the distance behind them he could make out a line of mangroves, with a stretch of tannin-soaked water between. The girl was maybe sixteen; the boy with her was a few years younger. He was shirtless, and had on a pair of cutoff jeans. She was in a modest, two-piece blue swimsuit. They both were smiling, tanned, and wore short, sun-bleached blond hair.

"Jason is my younger brother," she said, pointing to the lanky young man in the photo. "Well, my only brother. We were always very close. I guess, in a way, because I was older, he looked to me for support and guidance—something he never got from our mother. Growing up, Jason and I were never very close to our parents. They divorced when we were young, and once they did, neither seemed to have much time for us—so we depended upon each other."

Rehnquist studied the photo for a moment, then handed it back to Grace.

"When we were born our parents lived in a modest home in Coconut Grove. My father was an attorney who specialized in estate planning, and my mother . . . always the socialite. That all changed one day when the family of one of my father's clients came out on the short end when his estate was settled. Blackwell was his name. Julius Blackwell." Grace paused and took a sip of her wine.

"The old man had amassed a small fortune, and wanted to take care of his sons long after his death, and to make sure that next to nothing went through probate. His wife had died a few years before, and after she died, he hired my father to set up a living trust, into which he transferred most of his assets, equally distributed among his three sons.

"For a few years at least, my father apparently served Mr. Blackwell faithfully, and maintained the trust for him, buying, selling, and trading assets as he was instructed. Mr. Blackwell had worked hard all his life, and was a conservative investor. His only real concern was preserving the value of his sons' future inheritance. Any trading of assets was minimal, as were the fees generated for my father."

"Don't tell me . . ." Rehnquist interjected.

"Yep, you guessed it," Grace said, taking another sip of her wine. "As the years passed, Mr. Blackwell's physical heath began to fail, and he eventually ended up in a wheelchair. He died quietly one night in his sleep from an apparent stroke, but to the end, mentally, he was sharp as a tack. He never lost sight of his finances, and up until the moment he died, he knew what he was worth, and so did his oldest son—all of which was too bad for my father." Grace waived to Robyn for another Chardonnay. Robyn nodded, and pointed to Rehnquist. He shook his head, almost in disappointment.

"They say timing is everything," Grace continued. "For my father, I guess it was—or maybe just Karma. A month before Mr. Blackwell's death, my father had gotten himself into a little trouble gambling. He liked sports, and would bet on anything and everything. It began as a hobby, then it became an obsession. It seems that he had gotten himself in so deep, that he had blown through whatever savings he and Mom had, and was about to miss the mortgage payment, second month in a row. Then he remembered Mr. Blackwell. He could just borrow the money from the trust, earn it back on Sunday, and the old man would be none the wiser. Besides, he thought Blackwell owed it to him. By now Mr. Blackwell had stopped making any trades, and so my father was not making much of anything from the trust." Grace paused,

18

took the last sip of her Chardonnay, and slipped off her purse, sitting it on the chair beside her.

"Most of Mr. Blackwell's assets were in real estate or bonds, with a little in blue chip stocks, and a few hundred thousand in cash—money markets—just in case he needed the liquidity. The cash made it all too easy. Borrow a little now, a week later it would all be back, completely under the radar. When it came time for the monthly statement, the one with the two offsetting transactions, it would get lost in the mail. By the time the next month rolled around, the cash balance would have been restored, and that statement would have no record of the '*loan*.'"

"Nothing for you?" Robyn asked Rehnquist, when she brought Grace's Chardonnay, and picked up her empty glass.

"Water is fine for now," he said, "and I still have a little of this," retrieving the half-empty sidecar from the ice, "but I *will* take a Sam Adams with the burger."

"Sure thing," Robyn said, looking toward the service window. "I think it's up now. I'll be right back."

"*Beer?* What about your cholesterol?"

"Shit Grace, a man has to give into his vices every now and then," he said, as deadpan as he knew how.

Grace didn't look amused; she just went back to

her story. "Then Mr. Blackwell had to screw it all up by dying. *Oh*, and it didn't help that dear ol' Dad didn't win on Sunday. He lost . . . every cent."

"Ouch!" said Rehnquist.

Robyn returned with the food and Rehnquist's beer. "Anything else?"

"That should do it for now Robyn, thank you," Rehnquist said, with Grace nodding.

"It all came out at the trial. When the boys finally managed to get copies of all the brokerage statements and realized that the account was short an even one hundred thousand dollars, they knew right where to look. I can still remember the look on my mother's face when the cops knocked on the door, served the warrant, and took Dad away in handcuffs."

Grace took a bite of her salad, and washed it down with the Chardonnay. "My father pled guilty, and was sentenced to two years' probation and restitution, but he managed to stay out of prison. Of course he lost his license to practice law, and restitution required selling the house, which they probably would have lost anyway. By the time it was over it cost him everything, and Mom and Dad were broke."

Grace took a few more bites, picked at her salad, and then surrendered the fork, folding her napkin over it. "Ironic, isn't it? He couldn't pay the mortgage, so he stole money from a client, and ended up losing the house anyway . . . and everything else."

Sad story, Rehnquist thought, but he still had his appetite, and was quietly making his way through his burger and fries. "Tough on a marriage," he said, in-between fries.

"Yes, it was. Worse yet was when Mom found out about the blonde bimbo Dad was banging on the side. In addition to gambling . . . he had other addictions."

Rehnquist was silent now. *What could he say?* He took the last bite of his burger as Grace took another sip of wine.

"Not long after the divorce became final, Dad moved to Seattle to find himself, and to start a new life. That's when we pretty much lost contact with him. I haven't seen him in years, but the last time I did, he had let his hair grow to his waist, and he was working in some New Age shop in '*The People's Republic of Fremont.*'"

Rehnquist furrowed his brow and looked puzzled.

"Home of the counterculture."

Rehnquist just shrugged. Grace continued, "Hippies. Trolls, Lenin worshipers—"

"John?"

"Vladimir!" With a quick elbow to the ribs. Rehnquist yelped and pushed out his bottom lip. "Never heard of it . . ."

"You might like it. They have several breweries. Oh, and nude cyclists—"

"*Really?*" Rehnquist's pout turned into a grin and he cut her off. "Must go there sometime. Experience the '*counter*' culture . . . *Sorry*, and your mother?"

"She went off the deep end." Grace drained the last of her wine, and motioned to Robyn for one more. "She blamed herself. If she had been more of a wife, Dad wouldn't have needed to look outside the nest. She also knew about the gambling—but she had no idea just how bad it had become. But she still believed that if had she put her foot down when it first started, she could have changed him. Imagine that, a woman thinking she can change a man."

"You sound so cynical."

"I am," she said. "I've tried to change a few myself. The last one left me for his scrub nurse. But afterwards, he left me the house, the Mercedes, and half of everything else. After we were divorced, his scrub nurse left him. Guess I came out alright after all." She smiled and took a sip of water through her straw.

Rehnquist looked amused. *A woman scorned* . . . Robyn saved the moment with the Chardonnay, and

Rehnquist surprised her with a request for coffee. "A man has to know his limitations," he said, and laughed. Robyn smiled, and quietly took away his empty plate, and set off in search of coffee.

"Okay, back to your mom."

"What really killed her was losing the house. It wasn't all that impressive, but her parents had given them the money for the down payment. They both died in a car accident a few years later, and there she was, feeling like she had let them down, with no way to make it up to them." Grace struggled with this part of the story and for a moment, Rehnquist thought he saw the beginnings of a tear.

"We ended up in a small apartment in Redland. Mom was still a looker, and took a day job selling cosmetics at Macy's. At night . . . who knows where she went. She never told us—and we never asked—but we quickly figured out that she was on the prowl for the next Mr. Wonderful. We rarely saw her, but when we did, she'd talk about some great guy that she'd just met, and how she was sure that he could make her happy. Every once in a while she'd bring one home. It was always late, and Jason and I would be in bed asleep—at least until the noises started. *God*, it was awful."

"I'm sorry," he said, taking her hand. "No child should have to go through that."

Grace turned, looked into his eyes, and smiled. "Mom finally got her shit together, but the only man that was involved was Jesus."

"Really?"

"Really. I guess it was better for *her*, but for us, it was maybe worse. She went from having no interest in our lives, to driving us crazy. She wanted total control. She wanted to know where we were going, who we were going with, what time we'd be home—"

"You mean she became a mother."

Grace pressed her lips tightly together, and for a second, looked pissed. "Yeah, I guess so. But we'd never had one, so we didn't recognize it once we did. By then it was too late. And then there was *church*—twice a week, Sunday mornings and Wednesday nights, every week, and two nights of bible study. Of course she wanted us both to attend, but for the most part we refused. Of course that made us both heathen sinners."

Robyn returned with a carafe of coffee and two cups. "I thought *you* might like some too," she said to Grace.

"Yes, thank you. That would be nice."

Robyn poured two cups, set down a container of cream, a caddy filled with sugar and sweeteners, and disappeared into the shadows. For her age she was very perceptive. She could tell they'd be there a while.

Chapter Three

"School saved us from Mother," Grace said, adding a touch of cream to her coffee, and then offering it to Rehnquist. He shook his head.

"Just one sweetener please, a yellow one."

Grace handed him a packet, and took two for herself. Holding the tops, she shook them, tore them open, and poured all of one, and half of the other into her coffee.

"By the time Mother found Jesus, I had just started my junior year, and Jason was in eighth grade. We buried ourselves in our school work, and while she was off studying the bible, we were busting our asses studying anything that we thought might earn us a ride to college. Obviously Dad's calamity took away any hope of financial support from him or Mom, so that was the only hope we had."

Grace stirred her coffee, and as she lifted her cup, she smiled at Rehnquist. "Too bad we didn't play football," she said, half laughing at her own joke. She took a sip of coffee, then added a bit more cream.

"But you came out okay."

"We did. We both earned academic scholarships and we also worked weekends and evenings after classes." I majored in business, with the intention of going on to graduate school, but those plans were circumvented by my first future ex."

"Just as well," Rehnquist said, rolling his eyes. "Who needs an MBA anyway?"

Grace continued, "Jason graduated two years behind me, on an accelerated program."

"Easier classes?"

"No. Actually he majored in computer science with a minor in business administration, of all things. He was smart, real smart, *and*, he didn't have any distractions."

Rehnquist looked puzzled.

"Girls," Grace said, in answer to his bewilderment. "Oh, he had them, he just kept them at arm's length. A little dating. An occasional hookup. Nothing serious."

"And you know this how?"

"Jason would tell me."

"Your brother talked to you about his sex life?"

"Sure, why not?" Grace said, and shrugged.

Rehnquist dove for safer ground. "So, what's the connection—computer science *and* business administration? Couldn't decide what he wanted to do with his life?"

"No, that's just it. He knew exactly what he wanted to do." Grace suddenly looked startled, and stood up. "Please excuse me," she said, picking up her purse, "I need to visit the ladies' room."

As she walked away, Rehnquist wondered what had happened to her marriages. She seemed like a nice lady, and she carried an air of confidence. You could see it in the way she walked. She wasn't ashamed of her height—not that she should be—but he had known a few other women that were tall, and they always walked all hunched over, trying to make themselves look shorter. Unfortunately, it diminished not only their height, but also their character. Maybe it was because they were married to shorter men, who were embarrassed to have a wife that literally looked down on them. You'd never catch those women in a pair of heels, no matter the occasion. *I'll bet Grace wears heels . . . just not today, it wouldn't match the dress.*

Grace returned with fresh lipstick, and a renewed sense of purpose.

"Sorry, should have made that visit a while back," she said, looking embarrassed.

"It happens. Wine 'll do it to you every time. Sneaks up on you. Or, maybe it's the water," he said, smiling.

This guy was either a dick or a nice guy. She couldn't tell which, but in either case he put her at ease. "Where was I? . . . Oh yes, anyway, Jason's long-term plan was to design business software. More specifically, security analysis software. You know, stocks and bonds. I initially assumed that he wanted to write software and sell it commercially. He didn't. He wanted to write it for himself—to evaluate potential investments."

"More?" Rehnquist asked, pouring himself a second cup of coffee.

"Yes, just a little please."

Rehnquist filled her cup half full, just as Robyn made the rounds. "Can I get you anything else? Dessert, maybe?"

"You know, actually a shot of Kahlua would go great with this coffee," Grace said.

Robyn looked surprised, but beamed, "Now you're talking. How about you?" she said, turning to

Rehnquist.

"No, thank you. Just a little more coffee please," he said, handing her the near empty carafe.

Grace continued, "Not long after he graduated, Jason went to work in the IT department of Avonce Medical Billing. They were a small, but growing medical claims processor in Kendall. Since Jason was fresh out of school, it was a decent enough job, with a steady salary and great benefits. The company was doing well and expanding their customer base, and with it, their IT needs. Meanwhile, Jason was gaining experience and making his way up the ranks.

"Part of Jason's benefit package was the promise of future stock options when the company went public. He actually began to see a future for himself there— enough at least to put his long-term plans on hold. Everything was going great, up until after two or three years, when the company was quietly bought out by a competitor, and Jason and everyone else in his department was laid off . . ."

Grace trailed off, her words all but drowned out by the boisterous laughter at the high top, as the five boys stood and pushed in their chairs, each giving Robyn a big hug, and then waving goodbye as they made their way toward the door. Robyn waved goodbye, walked back to the bar, picked up her tray, and returned with the Kahlua and fresh coffee.

Knowing that they must have heard the ruckus, Robyn smiled at Grace and said, "My brother's friends," pointing toward the last one as he walked out the door. "When they're on break from school, they're regulars here. They're great guys."

As Robyn made her way back to the bar, Rehnquist suddenly became aware that he and Grace were the last patrons remaining in the dining room. He thought about it for a second, but then, this time, it was he who found the need to excuse himself.

"Grace, I'll be right back," he said, patting her shoulder as he left the table.

Grace poured the shot of Kahlua into her cup and stirred her coffee. *Well, at least I have his attention. Hopefully he'll understand what this means to me and agree to help me. If not, I don't know where else to turn.* She felt a tear slide slowly down her right cheek, and quickly brushed it away before it fell. *I have to keep myself together—for now. I can fall apart later.*

Jason was her rock. She had been through two marriages and one other serious relationship—all failed—and if she had learned anything from any of them, it was that Jason was the only man that she could really trust. He was her brother, but more, he was her best friend, and her confident. She could tell him anything, even things she couldn't, or wouldn't tell her closest girlfriends.

Rehnquist returned to find Grace staring down into her coffee. "You okay?" he asked.

Grace turned his way and smiled, "Just thinking about Jason."

"So, what happened after he was laid-off?" Rehnquist asked, sliding back into his seat.

"For a time he was really depressed, and even though he had never planned to work for any company long-term, he had really come to like his job and working there. Suddenly the job was gone, so was the paycheck, and the benefits. And the offer to purchase stock options? Gone. Cancelled when the deal closed. He felt betrayed by management."

"I can see why," Rehnquist said, "especially if he didn't see it coming."

"He didn't—none of the employees did. But he got himself together, and after a few months of unemployment he took a job at the Miami-Dade County School System, as a systems analyst. The job was fine, I guess. I mean it was okay for a while—and it paid the bills—but it wasn't much of a challenge, and Jason was bored. He took the job because he wasn't going to sit around on unemployment, and he wasn't yet prepared to delve into his software venture. At the same time, he continued his search for a more challenging job, but the economy and the job market was tight, and he couldn't find anything better—unless he moved out of state—which he wasn't willing to do."

Grace took a sip of water and looked back off into space, trying to figure out how to explain the rest of the story. Rehnquist waited patiently, giving her the time that she needed.

"Jason always had a strong work ethic, and even though he didn't like the job, he did his best—which was apparently good enough, because he was promoted two or three times after his first year of employment. But he needed more. After a while, his depression returned—a casualty of simply going through the motions every day. Then one day everything changed. He never explained why, but suddenly he was excited about going to work—as if every day were some new big adventure."

"Wow," Rehnquist said in surprise.

"He said that work was better; that he was happy. He gave up his job search, and once again put his future dreams on hold . . . Can you believe it?"

"Sounds . . . a bit bizarre."

Grace nodded. "This went on for the next couple years. Every time I talked to him, everything was great."

"And then?"

"He quit."

"Quit?"

"Yes, he quit. Out of the blue. One day he went in and put in his two weeks' notice, and that was that."

"Why?"

"He said that he had been working on developing his software, part-time, for the past couple of years. Supposedly he had reached some breakthrough and was ready to take it to the next step, whatever that means." Grace turned away, crossed her legs and folded her arms tight across her chest. "I didn't find out until a month *after* he quit. Jason told me everything, but he never told me about this. He never once mentioned that he had been working on a project, or that he was thinking of leaving his job, even though we saw each other regularly and spoke on the phone every day."

Wow, Rehnquist thought, not sure of what *to* say, or what *not* to say. He decided that he wouldn't say anything. Fortunately, Robyn looked his way, and his raised brow caught her attention. As Robyn approached, Grace briefly turned to glance back at Rehnquist and said, "A boy that will tell his sister about his sexual exploits doesn't hold back much, don't you think?"

Good point, Rehnquist thought, *good point.*

Chapter Four

"More coffee?" Robyn asked, as she approached their table.

"Actually Robyn, if it's not too much trouble, a nightcap would be nice," Rehnquist said. After three cups of coffee and this conversation, he was ready.

"No trouble—"

"I mean, if you need us to cash out, we can move to the bar," Rehnquist said, looking around the empty dining room.

"No, please. Relax. I'm here 'til close, and I have the bar tables too. And, believe it or not, sometimes we get busy, late. Now, what can I get you?"

Rehnquist looked at Grace. She was a bit more relaxed, but still tense. "I'll have a Beefeater tonic, please," Rehnquist said.

"Lime?" Robyn asked.

"Of course. Robyn, let me explain something to you. The essence of a gin and tonic *is* the lime. If anyone says no lime, or worse yet, they request a lemon, bring them vodka, they won't know the difference." Robyn giggled and turned to Grace who was once again staring off into space.

"Jim Beam, neat."

"Okay, I'll be right back," Robyn said. Looking to Rehnquist she mouthed, "Didn't see that coming . . ." He just looked bewildered and shrugged. *Me neither, and 'neat' to boot, sounds so refined.*

"Nick . . . I need your help," Grace said. After a moment, she slowly unfolded her arms, placed her hands on her knees, turned and made full eye contact with him. "Jason was—is—my everything. When we were little, we did everything together. We were inseparable. Because of the situation with my parents and their fucked up lives, we depended upon each other for survival. For years after we moved, we had very few friends our own age. Jason was my best friend, and I was his. His friends were my friends, and what few friends I had, were his. I guess this is unusual, but somehow it worked, and we all got along."

Grace picked up her purse from the neighboring chair and set it down in front of her. "Jason is smart, but he was never athletic, or strong. He's also four years younger than me, and when he was in middle school, he was bullied. I watched after him, and I've slapped the shit out of more than a few punks on the way home from school who decided to pick on the wrong kid. Another boy might have been humiliated, but not Jason. He thought it was funny. His big sis, kickin' ass. It didn't take long for the middle school hoodlums to learn to leave him alone."

Rehnquist smiled at the thought. Assuming that she was as tall in high school as she is today, she probably scared the shit out of them. Robyn arrived with the drinks, set them down, and then quietly, and quickly slipped back to the bar.

Grace opened her purse, reached into it, and pulled out a more recent photo, glossy with a thin white border, and handed it to Rehnquist. In this one, Grace and Jason were standing together, wine glasses in hand, toasting a moment in front of a tall Christmas tree. This looked to be a recent photo, perhaps taken within the past year. He looked at it for a moment, and then handing it back, he said, "Grace, I'd like to help you, but—"

"But, what?"

"I'd really like to help, but I don't do missing persons' cases. I mostly handle divorces, and insurance and workers' comp fraud. You need someone who specializes in these types of cases."

Grace threw back her Jim Beam and slammed the glass down on the table. "Bullshit! I need you!"

Rehnquist sat back quickly, startled by the unexpected response. Lowering his voice, he said, "I appreciate the vote of confidence, but why me Grace? For Christ's sake, I live in the Keys. I don't know shit about this area. I even had a hard time finding this place."

"Because we have a mutual friend who highly recommended you."

"A mutual friend? Who?"

"Captain George."

Rehnquist was thinking about anything but the Keys, and it took a moment to hit him. "George Weddle?" he asked, totally perplexed.

"George Weddle," Grace said, slowly letting go of her anger. "I've known him my entire life. That picture of me and Jason that you saw earlier was taken at George's house, back when he and Betty lived off Tarpon Basin. That flats boat was how he made his living back then—running backcountry charters. Of course that's before he bought the big boat and moved oceanside."

Clearly surprised, Rehnquist leaned forward. She had his full attention.

"George took that photo. We'd been out fishing all day. Another glorious day on the water." She closed her eyes and smiled in fond remembrance.

"I didn't know George back then," Rehnquist said. "I've only been in the Keys a few years."

"Oh, so you've only seen the big house."

"The big house? You mean the compound. Three acres, on the ocean—"

"Okay, so it's not a doublewide," she said, and they both laughed. "Actually, George inherited the property when his father died. That's where George grew up."

"How exactly do you know George?"

"George and my father were friends in college. They met during their sophomore year at FSU, and ended up sharing a small house off-campus their last two years. After they graduated, Dad headed off to law school, and George headed back to the Keys to fish and to marry Betty. He and Dad stayed in touch, and then after Dad finished law school and came back to South Florida, he and George got pretty close again. Dad met Mom in Tallahassee when he was in law school, and when he came back, she came with him. They got married a few months later, and George was the best man at their wedding."

Grace gave Rehnquist a moment to let reality sink in.

"Small world," he finally said. "You know, I've heard George talk about you and Jason before. Obviously, I didn't make the connection."

"Now you know. So, you and George are neighbors?"

Rehnquist laughed. "Not exactly. I live in a decent house down at Treasure Harbor a few miles away, but I wouldn't exactly call us neighbors."

"Well, George and Betty took a liking to us kids, and Jason and I used to stay with them over school vacations. George loved teaching us about the backcountry and how to fish, and Betty was much more a mother to me than my own mother ever was. Betty would have made a great mother . . . only she couldn't have children." Grace's smile turned to a frown.

"So you were close?"

"We still are—I guess. We just don't see each other very often." Grace paused, and momentarily drifted off, trying to collect her thoughts through the alcohol soaked haze. "They were there for us after my parents divorced. It was tough on both of us, but Jason took it really hard. He needed our father. Dad was never *much* of a father, and he was never really there, but suddenly he was gone, all but totally out of our lives. That's when

George stepped in. He gave Jason the support he needed, during the years that he needed it most."

Rehnquist nodded, he understood.

"I've never asked, but I don't think that George has ever forgiven my father—not for his legal or moral indiscretions—but for leaving his family. I do know that they haven't spoken in years." Grace reached for her purse, opened it, and retrieved another photograph. She handed it to Rehnquist. Like the first, this one was also without a border, but brighter and less faded. In this one the boy is at least sixteen, and he's grinning ear-to-ear, arms extended in front of him, and he's holding a bonefish which is at least thirty inches long. Behind him, with his arms wrapped around the boy's shoulders, is a beaming Captain George.

Suddenly Rehnquist got quiet, and his eyes got misty. "I've seen this picture before," he said, almost in a whisper. "There's a larger one framed in George's office, amongst a dozen or so others. I always assumed that he was a client's son." Rehnquist gave it a good, long look. "Where were you?" he asked.

Grace smiled, she had touched a nerve. "I was the photographer."

He slowly handed the photograph back to her. "Got any more?" he asked, secretly wishing there was.

"No, you're safe, that was the last one." Grace suddenly looked very tired and spent. The day had taken its toll.

"Grace, you weren't planning on driving back to West Palm tonight, were you?"

"No, I'm staying at Jason's, it's just off Palm."

Rehnquist looked down at his glass and took a moment to evaluate the situation. For once, just maybe, he'd be leaving the bar in better shape than his tablemate. He stood and signaled to get Robyn's attention, and once he had it, he held up his right hand and rubbed his thumb and index finger together, as if he were counting money. Robyn understood, and returned with the check. Over Grace's objections, without even looking at the bill, Rehnquist sent Robyn off with his credit card.

After a few minutes Rehnquist joined Robyn at the register. He talked with her for a moment and signed the check. She thanked and hugged him, and headed off to the telephone. After a few minutes she walked back to the table, nodded to Rehnquist, and said goodbye to Grace. They exchanged a hug, and Robyn said, "I hope to see you both again."

"I have a feeling you will," Rehnquist said. "Thanks again." As Robyn walked off, he took a final sip of his cocktail, which was now little more than water with a hint of lime and a few small floating chunks of ice. "Grace, we're both exhausted, let's call it a night."

Still standing, he bent over, reached behind her, and put his arm around her right shoulder. He pulled her into a half-hug and kissed her forehead. "Let me sleep on it, and I'll call you tomorrow. I promise I'll give it fair consideration; I just don't want to waste your time. Frankly, I don't know where to start." Grace just nodded in capitulation and laid her head on his shoulder.

"I don't even know Jason's last name."

"Roberts, same as mine."

"Oh, you changed yours back after your divorce."

"No, I never changed it to begin with," she said, lifting her head. "The name means something to me. I don't give a shit about my father, but this way, Jason, Mom, and I all share the same last name."

"I like that," Rehnquist said, smiling. He handed Grace her purse and helped her to her feet. "Okay now, you're in no shape to drive. Let's get you back to Jason's."

Chapter Five

The alarm went off at seven o'clock. Rehnquist was in a hurry to get home, but had purposely chosen to catch an extra hour's sleep. Last night when he paid the check, he asked Robyn to call a cab. Even though Jason's condo was just a few miles away, he knew that Grace had no business behind the wheel. He didn't either, but he was staying just down the street, and had planned on walking back to his hotel. He was prepared to do just that, but when he helped Grace into the cab, he felt obligated to make sure that she made it back to Jason's house safely. So he rode in the cab with her, walked her to the door, and once she was in for the evening, he had the cab driver take him back to his hotel. When he finally wound down for the evening, the last thought on his mind when his head hit the pillow was, *I hope Grace's Mercedes is still in the bar's parking lot in the morning* . . .

* * *

Rehnquist checked out of the hotel, threw his bag in the Mustang, and drove toward US 1. He had considered dropping the top, but reconsidered given the temperature outside, and the blazing morning sun, still low on the horizon. The deep blue GT muscle car was one of the few luxuries he gave into. For the most part he shunned material things, but he made an exception for that car. A few blocks later, curiosity—perhaps fear—got the better of him, and he began to worry about Grace's car. Not that Homestead was a bad place, or a high crime area, but it wasn't what it used to be—hell no place was.

He did a U-turn and drove back to Jake's and through the parking lot. When he saw a white Mercedes backed into a space next to the building, he let out a sigh of relief. It was still there, still had all four tires, and appeared untouched. For a moment, he felt better. Then, as he drove away and turned east toward US 1, an uneasy feeling came over him. He could only assume that the Mercedes he saw was Grace's. All he knew for sure was that at some point during the evening she said that she had a Mercedes, *and*, it was the only one in the lot . . .

By the time he hit the 18-mile Stretch, it was nearly 8:30, and he was later than he had planned. Fortunately, he was just late enough to miss most of the morning southbound commuter traffic from the mainland, and for the first several miles, traffic flowed smoothly. Then, just about five miles from the first passing zone, it slowed to a snail's pace. Rehnquist was usually patient, but not today. The situation really irritated him—not that he could do anything about it. When he reached the passing zone, he and a half dozen other cars in front of him quickly accelerated into the passing lane. About half a mile later he passed the vehicle responsible for the congestion. In typical Keys' fashion, it was a small, underpowered SUV with South Carolina plates towing a boat twice its size.

The remaining trip was smooth and uneventfully, other than he couldn't stop thinking about the previous evening's conversation, and what Grace had asked him to do: Find a man who one day suddenly dropped off the planet and apparently left no clue as to his whereabouts or why he left. As he approached the top of the Jewfish Creek Bridge, there wasn't a car for at least a half-mile behind him. Taking advantage of the unusual lull in traffic, he slowed down to where, for a moment at least, he could take his mind off last night long enough for a quick look. Off to his right, a lone sailboat under power had just emerged from beneath the bridge, making its way toward the marina at Gilbert's. To his left, looking far out over Barnes Sound, the sky was crystal clear, and off in the distance he could see the familiar sight of the Card Sound Bridge, and farther still, the cooling towers at the Turkey Point Nuclear Plant. By anyone's standards, it was a beautiful day.

A moment later, as he was approaching the end of the bridge, he crossed over Lake Surprise. The lake was empty, with the exception of a midsized sloop anchored just inside the entrance, and two kayakers. The wind was light, and the dark, tea colored water was flat, with only a ripple or two from an errant fish. As he crossed onto Key Largo, he took a deep breath, pursed his lips, and blew out a long sigh. For a time at least—he had left the mainland and the *real* world behind. Twenty-five minutes later, he was turning onto his street on Plantation Key, in the Village of Islamorada.

* * *

Rehnquist lived in a modest, two bedroom, two bath house on stilts. He had purchased the house from the bank four years earlier when it was in foreclosure. The first time that he saw it, he knew that it was the right house for him. Having lived most of his life in South Florida, he was concerned about storms, so he was pleased with the second story elevation and concrete construction. The house was also only a few years old, had decent appliances, and a modern, open layout. Fortunately, the previous owners had taken good care of it, and it didn't need anything beyond fresh paint in the living room and master bedroom.

The purchase price was also semi-affordable, as the house was on a dry lot, and it was for sale on the heels of the subprime mortgage debacle, at the same time the bank was trying to unload a hundred other properties in the Upper Keys. It also helped that he had made enough money off the sale of his house in the city that he could afford to carry the small mortgage and to pay for hurricane insurance.

Rehnquist maintained the presence of an office in his second bedroom, which doubled as a guestroom, although he rarely had guests. For some reason; however, he never really felt comfortable in the solitude of that room, and so he spent the majority of his office time on his laptop in his recliner, or at the kitchen table. Recently there hadn't been much office time, as jobs were few and far between, and he hadn't had an interesting or profitable case in over a month. So, in the weeks leading up to the call from Grace, asking him to meet her at Jake's to discuss the possibility of hiring him for an investigation, he had spent the majority of his time fly fishing, reading, and working on various projects around the house.

One regular, unintended, and uninvited guest that Rehnquist *did* have, was a sometimes friendly, sometimes not, feral calico named Hope. One day Hope just appeared from out of nowhere. Rehnquist pulled into his driveway, and sitting at the bottom of his stairs was a small calico cat with a left ear notch, the telltale sign of feral cat that had been trapped, spayed or neutered, and then released back into the wild. When Rehnquist got out of the car, the cat bolted, but over the course of the next week, he saw it at least a half dozen other times.

Rehnquist liked cats, but he was determined not to become attached to this one. Too many bad memories, and he believed that whenever he became attached to one, it never ended well. His first and only real pet was a cat. A black and white bicolored kitten with a black mask that he named Bandit, that was a birthday present from his parents on his sixth birthday. He loved Bandit, and for years she followed him faithfully around the house like a puppy. Then one day she stopped eating, and then drinking, became febrile and lethargic, and cried whenever he touched her. His mother drove him and Bandit to the vet, who diagnosed her with a kidney infection. The vet put her on antibiotics, and kept her overnight. In the morning, she was dead, and Rehnquist was heartbroken.

After that, he never wanted another pet, and it wasn't until a few years ago that he allowed himself to become attached to another animal; a male, orange tabby cat. Like this new little calico, it too was a feral that showed up under similar circumstances. He adopted it, and a month later it was killed crossing the street when it ran out in front of a car. So when this new friend came along, he swore to himself that he wouldn't feed it or do anything to encourage it to stay.

That all changed a few days later when it became apparent that the cat wasn't going anywhere, and

Rehnquist felt obligated to at least offer it a drink. It had been unusually dry for several days, so he set out a bowl of water on the top landing of his stairs. Once he went back inside the house, the cat came up to the bowl and started drinking. And so, with this simple act of kindness, Rehnquist allowed himself to become what he was determined that he would not—attached.

A few days later, he strengthened that attachment when he bought a bag of dry cat food and small matching food and water bowls. Later that day, when he sat out that first dish of food, he mumbled, "I hope you live longer than the last one. . . Hope . . . I'll call you Hope."

* * *

Rehnquist pulled under the house, grabbed his bag, and headed upstairs. He expected to see Hope, but she was nowhere in sight. That was not unusual, since she spent quite a bit of time down at the neighbor's, so he didn't give it a second thought. He unlocked the house and went inside. It was stuffy, so he kicked down the air, and then did a quick walk-though just to make sure that everything was all right—a habit that he had picked up years before, after coming home to a huge water leak. Everything was intact and in place—with no leaks.

By now the two cups of coffee that he had had earlier at the hotel was no longer cutting it, so he popped a pod of his favorite dark roast in the Keurig, made a cup of coffee, and sat down at the kitchen table and checked his email. Nothing but spam, and it made his wonder why he even bothered. As he sipped his coffee, he mulled over the possibilities, and tried to think of where he might begin if he decided to help Grace, and what his exit strategy might be, if he found himself just spinning his wheels. It didn't take him long to decide that other than Grace's hunch, he didn't have enough information to determine either. *So, what to do?* He looked at the time on his phone, 11:22. *Time to call George.*

George had given up the house phone several years ago when he and Betty entered the cellular age, so Rehnquist called George's cell, and he answered on the second ring.

"Morning George."

"Hey Nick, what's up?"

"George, we need to talk. Can I stop by?"

"You could, but I'm not home. I'm on my way back from Marathon. Where are you?"

"I'm home."

George looked at his watch. "It's almost lunch time, how 'bout you meet me in thirty minutes at the Lorelei? I could use a beer."

"Betty won't mind?"

"Naw, she's off shopping at Anthony's—they're having a three-day sale. She won't even miss me."

"Three-day sale? God help you."

"You're telling me. Now you see why I could use a beer."

"Definitely," Rehnquist said. "Alright, see you at the Lorelei."

Chapter Six

Marathon? Must be something pretty important going on in Marathon; otherwise George would never have been there. These days you couldn't get him past Bud N' Mary's, just south of the Lorelei, and you could only get him there because that's the marina where he kept his charter boat. George's boat was a beauty; a twenty-some-odd-year-old, 54' one-off that he bought reconditioned five years ago, and renamed for his bride of over forty years, 'Miss Betty.'

Rehnquist had plenty of time, but he left early as not to chance the drawbridge being up. Good thing. The bridge wasn't up, but southbound traffic had picked up considerably, and was much thicker than usual for a midweek September morning. Most times, this time of year, once the kids were back in school, most of the tourists were gone, and traffic wasn't a problem. Today it was.

Most of the Keys residents have a love-hate relationship with the tourists, and Rehnquist was no exception. You'd have to be a fool to live anywhere in the Keys and not recognize their contribution to the local economy. Tourism is after all, the number one industry from one end of the island chain to the other, and it keeps the county's unemployment rate at one of the lowest in the state.

Rehnquist's objections to the tourists were the same as everyone else, traffic. During peak vacation times, especially in and around Islamorada, it's all but unbearable. Both US 1 and the Old Road are packed, and with the backup from the drawbridge it can take an hour just to go ten miles. Worse than the traffic congestion is the erratic behavior of vacationing drivers, which is always predictably unpredictable: Driving fifteen to twenty miles under the posted speed limit; sudden stops, lane changes and turns; driving down the center turn lane; driving the wrong direction on the divided highway; and abruptly stopping on the bridges to look at the water. It's not surprising that there are so many accidents.

Today Rehnquist was lucky. Once he made it past Holiday Isle and over the Whale Harbor Bridge, he was on home stretch, and because he still had a few minutes, he stopped by the Islamorada Post Office to pick up his mail. It had been over a week and the box was overstuffed, mostly with advertising flyers and junk mail. By the time he had tossed everything that he didn't want or didn't need into the recycling can, he had the stack whittled down to a thank you card from a satisfied client, a credit card statement, and an envelope from the electric coop, addressed in red, which he didn't need to open. *Oops, better pay that.*

He got back in the car and threw the mail on the passenger seat, waited patiently until he had a safe break in the traffic, then pulled across the highway and turned southbound to go the final mile to the Lorelei. When he arrived, George was just pulling in, and Rehnquist pulled in right behind him. George managed to find a parking space up front; Rehnquist was not so lucky, and after circling the parking lot twice, he had to settle for a spot behind the bait shop next door.

George stood beside his truck and patiently waited for him to catch up. As they walked toward the restaurant Rehnquist pointed his left thumb over his shoulder at the parking lot behind him and said, "They're busy today."

George nodded. "Yeah, crazy for a Wednesday morning in September."

"You made good time. Were you still in Marathon?"

"No, I was on Grassy Key on my way back when you called."

"So, what's going on in the bustling City of Marathon?"

"County Commission meeting. They're considering a resolution to curtail mini-season in response to the public outcry after this last one."

"About time," Rehnquist said. Mini-lobster season was a never-ending bone of contention in the Keys. The hotels, convenience stores, dive operators, and some of the restaurant owners loved it for the income, but virtually everyone else hated it, and the destruction that it brought to the reefs.

"They had a hearing on it this morning. I wanted to weigh in."

Rehnquist didn't need to ask; he knew George's opinion.

"Bar Okay?" George asked, once they reached the restaurant. Like many of the restaurants in the Keys, the seating at the Lorelei is outside. The bar and surrounding tables are under cover; the deck, bridge, and beach tables are not. Since the bar is under cover, providing relief from the piercing sun, normally it would have been a good choice.

"Actually, I'd prefer the privacy of a high top if you don't mind."

"Okay, how about 'round the corner so we can look at the Bay?"

"Perfect."

As they walked around the short end of the bar, Rehnquist nodded to the bartender. A new guy. Rehnquist didn't know him. *Another one to train, like so many before him.* When they reached the other side, every high top was full. Several tables were available out on the open deck, but despite the table umbrellas, the few patrons out there were sweltering in the sun.

"Hmmm, that doesn't look like much fun," George said. "Back up front?"

"Lead the way."

They made their way back to the first round high top, the front table affectionately known as 'City Hall.' No sooner than they had set down they were greeted by the smell of familiar perfume, and a "Hey boys!" It was Chelsea, one of their favorites. She gave them each a hug and said, "Are you here for the lunch, or just to see me?"

"How about both," George said, "But let's start with a beer."

"Your usual?"

"Yes, please."

"And, what would your usual be today, Nick?"

Rehnquist thought about it for a few seconds, and said, "Let's start with an Imperil."

"Sure," Chelsea said, handing them each a menu. "It's been a while—it's great to see you both. I'll be right back."

Rehnquist looked back over his shoulder at the full tables. "I can't believe how busy we are for September, he said.

"I know."

Rehnquist thought about the traffic, the full parking lot, and all the full tables at midday. "It seems like we don't have a season anymore," referring to the usual seasonal ebb and flow of tourists.

"I would agree, but you'd never know it running a charter boat. Guess the economy's improving, but not enough that anyone wants to shell out the cash for a day on the water. Times like this I miss the backcountry. It was a lot easier to pull together a charter back then, and I didn't have to worry about whether or not my mate could afford to eat and pay rent."

"Speaking of mates, how *is* Jeff?"

"Good. He's a good man, and I'm lucky to have him. He's experienced, and he's also good with the customers. I even let him run the boat once in a while so

I can occasionally handle a line. That way I still remember how," George said with a smile.

Chelsea returned with the beers; Rehnquist's Imperial, and a Miller Lite for George. "Lunch?"

"Yes, please," George said. "Cracked Conch Sandwich with sweet potato fries."

"And for you? Chelsea asked, looking to Rehnquist.

"Buffalo wings, *smokin'* hot."

"That's all?" she said, collecting the menus.

"That's all," Rehnquist said.

As she was leaving, almost as an afterthought, Chelsea asked, "Two more beers?"

"With the food please," Rehnquist said, "only a Corona this time—NFL." George pointed to his bottle and nodded in agreement.

"I also picked up a part-time captain," George said. "Frank Osborn. He's new to the Keys, but worked running boats out of Miami for years. He's semi-freelance and runs a boat out of Robbie's two days a week, and the occasional six-pack out of Holiday Isle. I use him as a relief captain, when I need a day off. Nice guy, you'd like him."

Rehnquist took a sip from his beer and thought about how to begin this conversation. George was twenty years his senior, and he had more respect for him than he could ever express. He wanted to be careful not to offend, but he needed answers. "George, I received a call from an acquaintance of yours."

"You don't say?"

"As if you didn't know . . . Please, tell me about Grace, and Jason, and their family."

"Sure, what do you what to know?"

"Family dynamics, relationships—your perspective. Anything that might help me understand them a little better."

"Okay."

George spent the better part of the next hour talking about his college days and his friendship with Stephen Roberts, and how their friendship continued through law school, marriages, and the birth of the kids; the downfall of Stephen Roberts and his divorce from Mimi, and about the years George spent with Grace and Jason on the water. His story, although more detailed, paralleled everything that Grace had told him the night before. Midway through the conversation Chelsea brought the food.

"Cracked Conch with sweet potato fries, and buffalo wings," she said, sitting the baskets down in front of them. I'll be right back with your beers." No sooner than Rehnquist realized that he didn't have cutlery, she was back, cold beers in hand.

"Chelsea, could I trouble you for a knife and fork?"

"Sure, I'm sorry, I forgot. I'll be right back."

George looked at him incredulously. "For Chrissakes Nick, who the hell eats wings with a knife and fork?"

"I do—you know that. Every civilized man does. I don't touch my food. Occasionally French fries, and maybe pizza, if it's not drippy. That's all."

"Jesus, that's just weird."

Chelsea brought them each a knife and fork rolled in a napkin. George unrolled his, set his knife and fork aside, and put his napkin on his lap. He dipped a French fry into a mound of catsup, and then watched Rehnquist with disdain as he filleted his first wing, skillfully cutting the meat off in two strips, with only a spot of gristle left on one end of the bone.

"Fry? George asked."

"Sure," Nick said, as he plucked one from George's basket with his fork.

"But you said . . ."

"I said occasionally, but not today . . ."

After a brief pause, the conversation returned to Grace and Jason.

"Alright then, if we're finished discussing my culinary habits, do you really believe that something happened to Jason? No chance that he didn't just decide to escape from life for a while?" Rehnquist asked.

"Yes."

"Yes, what?"

"Yes, I believe that something has happened to him." George said.

"Really? Have you told Betty?"

"No, I can't. That's where you come in."

"You expect *me* to tell her?"

"No, I expect *you* to find him."

"Thanks George," *no pressure here.* Rehnquist plucked another French fry from George's plate. "Okay, tell me about Grace."

"What do you want to know?"

"The real story. What's she really like? What about the husbands?"

"The woman you met last night is the real deal. That's Grace. She is exactly who she seems to be, with no pretense. Why are you asking? You're not getting sweet on her, are you?"

"George . . ."

"If you are, I'm thinking you're too old. She's a good 10 years younger."

"George . . . the husbands."

"Jerks, both of 'em, as was the other ass she lived with for a couple years. If the woman has a single flaw, it's having poor taste in men. Understand? When it comes to love, the woman is a shit magnet."

"I get it George. I've known a few in my younger years, and just hoped that I wasn't the piece of shit that they were attracted to."

"Not likely Nick, not likely." George killed his beer and said, "Let's settle the check and go back to my house. I have something I want to show you."

"Okay," Rehnquist said and nodded. They called Chelsea over to the table, then split the check down the middle, each leaving a generous tip.

"George, before we go, why did you recommend *me?*"

"Because I know you. I believe in you, and I believe that you can help her—that you can help us."

"Why didn't you give me a heads up?"

"Because she asked me not to."

"So?"

"The lady made a fair request. You spent a little time with her, what would you have done?"

Rehnquist thought about it for a moment, raised his brow and shrugged. It was hopeless. "One last question, what did you tell her about me?"

"Just that you're a good friend, and a highly decorated, retired veteran detective of the City of Miami Police Department."

"Nothing more?"

"Nothing more."

Chapter Seven

Rehnquist followed George north on US 1. At Treasure Harbor Drive, just a few streets south of Rehnquist's house, they turned onto the Old Road and drove the remaining couple of miles to George's house. George hit the remote and opened the gate at the entrance to the compound that was once his parent's home. He drove through the gate and Rehnquist followed, and the gate closed behind them. As they came around the corner and pulled up to the main house, George pulled under the house next to Betty's car, and Rehnquist pulled in under the shade of a large Mahogany in the drive.

As Rehnquist opened the door to get out, George pointed up to a bright patch of green on a branch of the tree and said, "If I were you, I'd wouldn't park there, unless you want your car covered in iguana shit. I made that mistake a week ago when I was pressure washing the carport."

"Thanks," Rehnquist said, and pulled out of the shade and parked in the sun behind George.

Good choice, George thought. *Now all you have to worry about is birds.*

Rehnquist closed his car door and pointed to Betty's car. "She's early, must not've been too good a day for shopping."

"That or too good," George grumbled. "A month ago I told her, you keep shopping and I'll cut off your cards."

"What'd she say?

"She said, 'You cut off the cards, I'll cut off something else.'"

Rehnquist grabbed his crotch and yelped, "Well, since I saw you stand up and pee before we left the Lorelei, I'm guessing she still has her cards . . .'"

"Funny, smart ass. Let's go inside so you can say hi to Betty, and then what I want to show you is out in my office."

Rehnquist followed George upstairs and through the front door where they were greeted by Betty with outstretched arms. "Nicky, so good to see you."

"Good to see you too, Betty," he said. He pushed his sun glasses up on his head and gave her a big hug. "How was shopping?"

"Good. I found some nice dresses—not in my size—but they're going to order them for me. They'll be in next week."

"Greeeeeaaat." George snarled.

"You be still, old man." Betty was still standing, facing Rehnquist, and she took hold of his hands. "Nick, how have you been?"

"Alright. I'm staying busy—I guess that's good."

"Can I get you two something to drink?" Betty asked.

George said, "Thanks, but I have something I want to show Nick out in the office. We'll grab a beer there."

"Okay. Well, it sounds like you boys have something to talk about, I'll let you be. Nick, give me another hug."

She hugged him, and as they broke their embrace she looked into his eyes at the dark circles and bags underneath. "Nick, you look tired. You're not getting enough rest."

Rehnquist just shrugged his shoulders and frowned. "I am tired; guess I'm not sleeping very well."

"Well I worry about you. You know what they say about all work and no play?"

"Yes I know," he replied, half-smile replacing his frown.

"Are you seeing anyone?"

"No Betty, and I can't imagine that I ever will."

"I know Nicky, but I had to ask."

As he and George turned to leave, Betty said, "Nick, how about dinner—fresh fish?"

"I'd love to, but not tonight. I'm working on a case—at least I think I am. Another time?"

"Anytime. You're always welcome."

Rehnquist followed George out the back door onto the balcony, down the back stairs, and across George's well-manicured lawn toward his office. George was very proud of his lawn—so few homes in the Keys had one. Rehnquist certainly didn't. He, like most everyone else, had pea rock. George had put that sod in several years ago and had spent a small fortune on the installation and maintaining it. A lot of effort and a ton of money, but Rehnquist had to admit that it was absolutely beautiful.

George's inner sanctum was in a small, two-room, wood framed structure with a half bath that sat at the foot of his dock with its long extended pier. The back room was mostly storage, but the front room was a beautiful office that overlooked the open Atlantic Ocean. Everything about the room was inviting. His desk was handmade from Cuban Mahogany with matching bookcases and a credenza, and they were surrounded by well-accented wall and floor coverings of teak and bamboo.

George wasn't fishing as much as he used to, so he spent quite a bit of time in his office these days, writing his memoirs and a book on the history of Florida Keys fishing. Since he had no children to carry on the family name, he wanted the fishing book to be his legacy.

They walked in and Rehnquist took a seat in an overstuffed armchair next to George's desk, and began thumbing through a copy of 'Florida Sport Fishing.' "How about a beer Nick? I think I've still got a few of the Presidentes you left the last time you were here; if not, I always have Miller Lite.

Without even looking up from the magazine, Rehnquist said, "I prefer beer, thanks. I'll have a Presidente." George grimaced at the insult and looked down over his glasses at Rehnquist. Once George turned to walk to the refrigerator in the back room and it was safe, Rehnquist flashed an impish grin.

Rehnquist heard George pop the tops off two bottles, then he returned with the beer. He handed a cold Presidente to Rehnquist, set his Miller Lite down on his desk, and threw Rehnquist a faded Lorelei koozie.

"Thanks buddy."

George raised his bottle in salute, pointed to a framed photo on the wall, then turned to his prized wall of fame, where he had memorialized the highlights of many a day's fishing charters. "I know you have seen this picture, but how about these?" he asked, pointing to three photographs pinned among several dozen others on a corkboard. Rehnquist stood for closer examination. All three were of George and Jason taken over a period of several years.

"No, I never really noticed."

George walked past Rehnquist to the double bookcase. "Here's what I brought you here to see," he said, reaching for a well-worn, leather-bound photograph album. George pulled up a folding chair next to Rehnquist and they spent the next hour, and the next beer, looking at pictures. There were a few early photographs of George and Betty and Grace's parents, but most of the photos were of Grace and Jason. George could remember the day and the story behind each of the photographs, as if it were yesterday. These were happy times. Time spent on the water. Time spent fishing.

Time spent with surrogate children. The last photos ended just about the time the kids went off to college.

George closed the book and looked very sad. "I always hoped one day to start Volume Two with the next generation, but that doesn't look like that's going to happen anytime soon. George took a lengthy pause and another sip of beer. "Jason and I were very close for many years. Even throughout high school he would call once or twice a week. Once he was in college, he called less often and the visits became increasingly infrequent— even more so after he graduated—but I guess that's the norm for children. I know it was for me, and I only lived a few miles from Mom and Dad," he said, looking up to a portrait of his parents on the wall above his desk. "One more by the water?" he asked, pointing toward the window.

"Sure."

George grabbed two more beers and they went out and sat down on Adirondack chairs in the shade of a chikee, staring out at the open water. The tide was high and just beginning to ebb, with a light breeze from the east, and although it was almost 90°, they were more than comfortable. The late afternoon sun was now behind them, and even though it would not set for several hours, the rising moon was already clearly visible on the horizon in the cloudless sky. They sat in quiet contemplation, watching a lone frigatebird soaring high in the distance, until a laughing gull broke the silence with its call.

"What are you gonna do Nick?" George asked.

"What do you think I should do?"

George laughed. "What the hell kind of question is that? Didn't I send Grace your way?"

"Yeah, I guess you did."

Rehnquist sat quietly for a while watching the outgoing tide, his energy going with it. Finally, he drained his beer and said, "Well, I guess I better get going, I've got a busy week ahead."

Chapter Eight

Rehnquist drove home, and still no Hope. In anticipation of her late-evening return, he freshened up her water and put out a scoop of food, and then collapsed on the couch. He hadn't slept well the night before, and he was exhausted. Not quite ready for sleep, he turned on the TV and began flipping channels: Late afternoon soap operas and talk shows; self-help and advice shows; weight loss programs; court shows and 'real life' crime docudramas; infomercials, and a handful of reality TV shows. *Jesus, no wonder I never turn on the TV until late evening.* He drifted off during a PBS documentary on the building of the pyramids, and woke up feeling anything but rested somewhere past eight.

He got up and went to the bathroom, and on his way back to TV land, he grabbed a Sam Adams Octoberfest from the refrigerator that was as empty as he'd ever seen it. After a few moments of listening to his stomach growl, he came to the realization that he was hungry, and went in search of sustenance. He didn't want to go back out, and he wasn't in the mood to cook—which really didn't matter, because there was nothing *to* cook. *Guess eventually, I'm gonna have to break down and go to the store.*

He could always settle for the bag of stale chips on the counter, the freezer burnt boiling bag of mixed vegetables, or the assortment of leftovers in his refrigerator: a box of pork fried rice that resembled a seventh grade science experiment, a long forgotten half-Cuban sandwich from the Sunrise Market, or four slices of a more recent Boardwalk pizza still in the box. At least he had plenty of beer. He eventually settled for two slices of cold pizza, straight out of the box, and even ate it with his hands. *If only George could see me now.*

With a full belly, and after another beer, he was ready to face the inevitable, and picked up his phone. She either expected his call or she was holding her phone when he called, because she answered on the first ring. "Hello Grace."

"Hello Nick."

"I spent the day with George."

"How's he doing? I spoke with him on the phone the other day when he recommended you, and a few days before when I told him about Jason, but I haven't seen him in a while."

"He's doing well. The bad hip's got him moving a little slower, and he's not fishing as much as he used to, but he and Betty are heathy, and seem to be enjoying life. He's very worried about Jason though."

"I know. Did he tell Betty?"

"No, and he doesn't plan on telling her. He said that's where I come in. I said, 'You expect me to tell her?' and he said, 'No, I expect you to find him.'" Rehnquist sighed, paused, and took a sip of beer. "That's why I'm calling, Grace. I've thought it over. I'll help. I'll do my best to find your brother."

The phone was silent for several seconds, then Grace responded. "Oh my God Nick, thank you."

"Thank me when—if—I find him. I'd like to meet with you sometime tomorrow to discuss particulars and to get some more information about Jason. Are you available?"

"Pick a time, and I'll *be* available."

He thought about it for a second—how long it would take him to get himself together, take care of a few things at home, and drive up to Homestead. "How about nine—no, ten o'clock?"

"That's fine Nick, and if you're early, I'll be ready."

"Okay, meet you at Jason's?"

"Yes, certainly."

"I know I was just there, but please text me the address. It was dark, and I'll never find it on my own."

"Okay."

"Alright, see you then."

"Goodbye Nick, and thanks again.

"See you tomorrow Grace."

Rehnquist hung up the phone, picked up his beer, and moved over to his recliner. Within a minute Grace texted him Jason's address, and he pulled it up on Google Maps. *Good thing I asked . . .* He played over the events of the past day in his mind, then picked up a pen and legal pad from the end table beside him and made a few notes. Then he began to make a list of where he needed to take the conversation tomorrow, and what he wanted to ask Grace.

Halfway through the list the day caught up with him, and he surrendered to an uneasy sleep. As he fell, deeper and deeper into the abyss from which he could never fully escape, he began to relive the same hellish nightmare that he had had so many times before. He could hear her softly calling his name—then screaming for help. He awoke in a cold sweat, heart pounding, and breathing heavily, calling her name aloud.   It was his fault . . . he let her go. It should have been him. She never should have been there. If only . . .

Once he regained his composure, he decided that the rest of the list could wait until tomorrow, and dropped the legal pad onto the floor. He walked to the kitchen, tossed his bottle into the recycling bin, and pulled a clean Old Fashioned glass from the hutch that served as his makeshift bar. He filled it with ice and three fingers of Grey Goose, and still thinking about tomorrow, packed a bag with toiletries and enough clothes to last a few days—just in case. Once the bag was packed and the Goose put to bed, he decided to call it a night—hopefully without another nightmare.

Chapter Nine

Rehnquist's alarm was set for six, but he was up by five thirty, wide awake and ready to go. He threw on a pair of gym shorts and a running shirt, a sport watch and his iPod shuffle, and headed out for an early morning run. He wasn't really in the mood for it—he was more of an evening runner—but he knew that if he didn't go now, he wouldn't get the chance to run later. He stepped out into the thick early morning air, salt heavy on his skin, and the smell of Night Blooming Jasmine wafting from the neighbor's yard next door.

Although it was still quite dark, he chose to stick to the Old Road. The bike path alongside US 1 might have been safer, but the Old Road was fairly well lit, he was wearing a reflective shirt, and at the time of day, there was almost no traffic.

Once he got going it was an easy run, the light breeze from the east keeping both the heat, and the mosquitoes at bay. He ran north, turned around at the high school and ran back home, completing his run of just over six miles in under an hour. He wasn't happy with his time, but considering that he was tired and half hungover, he'd take it. Climbing to the top of the stairs, Rehnquist was greeted by Hope. She had apparently finally decided to come home, and was purring and glad to see him. He bent down to pet her, but thought better of it as he was dripping wet with sweat and would come back with a handful of fur.

He retreated inside to the air conditioning, toweled off and wiped the sweat from his face and arms. He washed his hands at the kitchen sink, and went back outside to pet Hope, give her fresh water, and since he wasn't sure that it was her—and not the night roving neighborhood raccoons—that ate her food, he gave her another half scoop. Hope purred and arched her back high against the pressure of his hand as he stroked her back. "Guess you need me girl, as much as I need you," he said, as he gave her a final scratch under her chin. "Since you'll most likely be gone when I leave, I guess this is probably goodbye."

Rehnquist went back indoors, downed a bottle of water from the refrigerator, and brewed the day's first cup of coffee. Then he shaved off a greying two-day stubble, showered, and while he sipped his coffee and ate a protein bar, he pressed the wrinkles from his choice of the day's clothes: navy cargo shorts and a white Tommy polo. While he brewed a second cup to go, he slipped into his clothes, and into a pair of navy boat shoes with matching belt. He fired up his laptop, logged on and paid a few bills, including the overdue one from the electric co-op. Next he quickly checked his emails, and then shutdown the laptop and bundled it up along with his iPod, which he brought along just in case he ended up spending the night, and had the chance to run tomorrow morning.

He loaded up his electronics, camera with a selection of lenses, and the bag that he had packed the night before into the Mustang. He went back up for his coffee, and made one last check to make sure that he had shut off all the lights and the water wasn't running in either bathroom. On his way out he remembered to grab his running shoes and cell phone charger, locked the door, and said a second goodbye to Hope, who was still loitering at the front door. If he did end up being gone for a few days, she'd be fine, stealing an occasional meal from the neighbor's cats next door.

On his way to the mainland, Rehnquist stopped for gas just before he left Key Largo. By now the sun had been up for over an hour and it was a sticky 82 degrees. It was going to be another hot one, but he still had the light easterly breeze, and when he stepped out from under the gas station canopy, he realized just how nice the sun felt on his face and arms. He decided to enjoy it a bit longer, so he dropped the top on the car for the ride north, and then headed up the Stretch.

Chapter Ten

"Good morning Nick."

"Hey Grace. I'm on way up. I just passed the county line, almost to the first passing zone."

"You're early," Grace said, sounding surprised. "Good."

"Figured I'd better get an early start; I have a feeling it's going to be a busy day. I hope I'm not too early."

"No . . . I'm just finishing my coffee and getting ready to get in the shower. I should be finished in plenty of time."

"Okay, see you in a bit."

* * *

Once he turned onto Palm Avenue at Florida City, Rehnquist followed his phone's directions to Jason's complex. When he arrived at the entrance, he rang Grace and she let him through the gate. As he drove into the parking lot he saw Grace's Mercedes pulled into a numbered parking space in front of Jason's unit. He parked two rows behind, in a space marked 'VISITORS.' After he put the top up on the car, he tossed his overnight bag in the trunk, and then grabbed the bag with his computer and electronics and his photography equipment and headed upstairs. As he walked by Grace's car he took note of her UM vanity license plates, 'DGR.'

Rehnquist rang the doorbell twice before Grace answered. When she opened the door she was wrapped in a white towel, and running a second towel through her hair. "I'm sorry," she said. "My mother called and I couldn't get her off the phone. Come on in." Motioning toward the living room she said, "Please have a seat, I'll be just a minute." Rehnquist was glad she didn't linger. Not that she didn't look good in a towel—she did—but to say that it made him feel uncomfortable was an understatement.

The front door opened into a small foyer, and in typical condo fashion, the living area was open, a high top breakfast bar with two chairs separating the kitchen from the living room. The kitchen had a small dining area off to one side with a round table and four chairs, and the barest counters he'd ever seen.

The living room was furnished with an off white, L-shaped leather sectional, with the sofa portion pressed tight against the solid wall, and the loveseat pulled back into the room to allow egress behind onto the balcony. Turned diagonally, next to the loveseat, was a matching recliner, with an octagonal end table with a dark, honey pine finish in-between. On top of the end table was a simple brass lamp and a framed 8x10 photo of Jason, Grace, and their parents in front of the Cinderella Castle at the Magic Kingdom, taken when the children were quite young. Grace was standing in front of her mother, Mimi's hands resting on her shoulders, and Stephen was holding Jason, who couldn't have been more than a year old. *Happier times, before the old man fucked it up.*

At the far end of the sofa was another octagonal end table, with a second brass lamp that was pushed far to the back. In front of the lamp was a large, handcrafted brass sloop, mounted onto a flat piece of highly polished driftwood. Rehnquist recognized the sloop. These ships are highly detailed one-offs made by master craftsmen, and are fairly rare. Captain George had one of these in *his* living room—hardly a coincidence.

The rest of the room was rather Spartan, with the exception of a sixty plus inch TV mounted on the wall, and a medium size framed painting of the Everglades. From all appearances, Jason kept clutter to a minimum.

Rehnquist placed his bag on the floor and then sat down on the loveseat next to the table with the photo of the Roberts family.

"Coffee Nick?" Grace asked, as she came into the room. She had slipped into a pair of tight khaki capris, and a white half sleeve crop top pullover with matching flip-flops. Her still wet hair hung loose on her shoulders.

"Yes, please."

Rehnquist followed her to the kitchen where she poured two cups from an ancient Mr. Coffee. She handed him a cup and smiled, "Sorry, you'll have to settle for one blue."

"That'll work."

They walked back to the living room, and Rehnquist returned to his original seat and Grace sat down beside him. She looked better today, more rested, and if possible, her eyes a bit bluer. They were almost startling, really, and it made him wonder if the color was enhanced by contacts. She wore no makeup, not even lipstick, but she was still beautiful. And, there was no trace of perfume today, just the delicate fragrance of her freshly washed hair, a suggestion of body wash, and a trace of fabric softener in her clothes.

"Grace, I have a lot of questions, and I'd like to take notes if that's all right."

"Yes, of course."

Rehnquist reached into his bag and pulled out the legal pad onto which he had scribbled his list of questions the night before. "To begin with, I need to know as much as you can tell me about Jason's job with the school system: when he started, positions he held, anyone that you may have met that he worked with, and anything that he may have told you about his sudden departure."

"I'm not really sure what Jason did at the billing company, but I know that he found it interesting and challenging—at least he said he did. His first job at the school system was anything but—he said that it was grueling and incredibly repetitive. He was an entry-level systems analyst, and basically he ordered and setup new computers, installed software and maintained updates. He also reset passwords when people locked themselves out of their computers—which he said was often. He said that the most important part of his job was protecting users from themselves, because most computer users come in one of two categories: either incredibly stupid, or they think they know more than they do, which is just enough to get them into trouble. He said there's a reason why, when you call a computer help line, that they begin by asking you if the computer's plugged in."

Rehnquist smiled. "I'd like to think that I'm reformed now, but one of those two categories used to describe me."

Grace nodded, smiled, and pointed to the center of her chest. "Guilty as charged; both counts," she said, and they both laughed.

Grace continued, "Jason's first promotion was to move up to a second level of systems analyst. He said the job was basically the same, just a little bit more administrative responsibilities, a small a raise, and the recognition of having completed his first year on the job. He was still bored to death."

Rehnquist listened attentively, and wrote down the occasional chicken scratch. He wasn't sure why. His handwriting sucked, and he could never read his notes. He should have just recorded her, but recordings always seemed intrusive.

"A year or so into that job, Jason had the opportunity to move up to network administrator. After he got his degree, Jason had continued his education at night with online classes, and he wanted to learn more about networks. The position offered him a new challenge, and when he got the promotion he thought that it might be something that he would really enjoy. It did come with a nice pay raise, but soon he was as bored as he was before, and more frustrated than ever. He said the school system's network was antiquated and slow, and even though they were willing to spend a fortune on classroom computers, he had a hard time getting the money to make network repairs, let alone upgrades. During this time Jason continued his job search, hoping to find something better. Then, about a year into that position, his attitude totally changed."

Grace stood up and walked to the front window. She opened the blinds and looked out, down onto the parking lot below. "Nice car."

"Thank you," Rehnquist said, smiling. "That was my midlife crisis."

"The Mercedes was mine," Grace said, and then turned around to face him and returned the smile. "Bet it's hard to do surveillance work in that."

Rehnquist laughed. "It would be, but I also have a Key's beater, a fifteen-year-old black F-150 with heavily tinted windows."

"That's inconspicuous?"

"It is in the Keys. It seems like everyone has a truck to tow their boats, and black Fords outnumber the rest by a mile."

"Oh, right, guess I never thought about it," Grace said, as she sat back down. "Jason and I talked together on the phone every day, but our calls were usually short, just checking in on one another, or talking about Mom and whatever craziness she'd been up to. Then, once or twice a week, we'd get together for dinner. Sometimes Jason would drive up to West Palm and meet me; other times I drove down here and met him. Either way we'd get to talking old times and invariably end up spending the night at one another's houses. Anytime Jason and I were together, he rarely talked about work, unless I asked, and whenever I did, it was always the same. Bored, frustrated, and looking for a way out."

Grace paused and took a sip of coffee. "One night Jason met me for dinner at the Capri, over on Krome."

Request nodded and said, "I know where it is, I've been there many times."

"I arrived there early and was having a glass of wine at the bar. Jason snuck up behind me and gave me the biggest hug. He looked the happiest I'd seen him in the longest time. I gave him a kiss and said, what's up? He said, 'Not much sis, what's up with you?' He had a shit-eating grin, and gave me that sort of, if you really want to know, you'll have to pry it out of me look. I decided I'd wait until dinner to see if I could get him to tell me just what he was so happy about. Jason ordered a cocktail—his usual, a vodka tonic—then we transferred the tab over to our table.

"We ate at the Capri often. We almost always had the same server—by request—and she came over immediately to take our order. Not that we were in any hurry to eat, it's just that we didn't need menus. We rarely ventured off the beaten path, so there was no decision making. After she brought us our wine and we placed our order, I asked Jason how work was going. I fully expected that I'd get the usual answer, and then I could ask him what was going on his personal life that put him in such a good mood. Long story short, he said that everything at work was great, that it had never been better. Imagine my surprise."

"So what changed?" Rehnquist asked.

"Who knows," Grace said with a shrug. "When I asked him, he said, 'I don't know, maybe it's me, maybe I just stopped looking at the negatives. You know, the power of positive thinking.' And that was pretty much it. At the time I felt that there was more to the story—and I still do—but I wasn't going to pry."

"That's it, he didn't give you anything specific?"

"Nothing. He just changed the subject. Time to talk about Mom, and that was that."

"How was he after that?"

"Every time I talked to him on the phone, or at dinner, he was upbeat and positive. After a while I actually began to believe that he was enjoying his job and what he was doing—that is, until he quit."

"And you said that he didn't tell you at first—"

"Not for a month—even though I talked to him every day—and not even when we met for dinner. In fact, I'd ask him, 'How's work?' and he'd say 'great.'"

"With a straight face?"

"Totally. Then after a month, he dropped the bomb. I met him for dinner, and then we came back here. He poured us a glass of wine, and once we were relaxed, sitting right here, he said, 'Sis, I have something to tell you. I left the school system, and now I'm self-employed.' I was beside myself. Especially when I found out that it had been a whole month—"

"What'd you say?" he interrupted.

"I guess he just expected me to be happy for him—and maybe I could have, if he had given me a heads up before he quit, or at least once he did."

"So, what *was* your reaction?"

"I was hurt, there was no hiding it. Instead of congratulating him, I lit into him. I said, 'Why didn't you tell me sooner, before you quit?' Jason told me that he loved me, and that I had always been there for him, to guide him and help him to make the right decisions, but this was one decision that he had to make on his own, and that's why he didn't tell me, or anyone else. That way, win or lose, it was his choice. He said that he still hadn't told anyone else, including Mom."

"Did you believe him . . . about needing to make his own decision?"

"I don't know. I guess I did at the time. I mean, it made sense. Look, for years I was Jason's sister, but I was also his mother. I offered my advice whether he asked for it or not. When he said that this was a decision that he had to make for himself, it hit me, maybe sometimes I was over the top, and I actually felt guilty."

Rehnquist sat forward on his seat and put down his legal pad. He had long since quit taking notes. "So, what happened?"

"I hugged him, and told him that I understood, and that I supported his decision. Then, in the days and weeks that followed, whenever I talked with him on the phone, or over dinner, he said things were going well, and that he was very happy with his decision."

"So, he seemed happy."

"Yes, everything seemed fine. The last time I saw him was on Friday night, now almost three weeks ago. We had dinner—at the Capri—and then we came back here. We rented a movie, made popcorn, and nothing seemed out of the ordinary. I left mid-afternoon on Saturday and went back home. I talked to him on Sunday morning, and then every day until Thursday. Jason usually called me first in the mornings, and that day he didn't call. I called him, but he didn't answer, so Wednesday evening was the last time I talked to him."

"When he didn't answer, what'd you do?"

"I called, I texted, then I freaked out—it was so unlike him. So I drove down. His car wasn't here and he didn't answer the door, and so I let myself in—obviously I have a key. Everything in the house was in order. The bed was made; the dishes were washed—nothing was out of place. I'm not sure about his clothes, but as far as I can tell, all of his luggage is here."

"Did you call your mother?"

"Of course. She hadn't heard from him either. These days Jason is fairly introverted and doesn't have many friends, and I don't have any contact information for the few that he has, so there was no one for me to call. I slept here Thursday night, and then Friday morning, after Jason didn't return home and I still couldn't reach him, I called George. On Saturday, I got so desperate that I called our father. Can you imagine? Listening to him talk you would have thought that we were the closest of families. Pathetic bastard. He hadn't seen or heard from Jason, but promised to call if he did. It was at that point that I called the cops."

"Who'd they assign the case to?"

"Wait, I have a card," Grace said. She got up, walked back to one of the bedrooms, and returned with her purse. "Ever heard of this guy?" she asked, handing Rehnquist a business card.

Rehnquist took the card and studied it for a moment. It was a standard generic police department card with the name of the detective and his office number printed on it, and a case number written across the top in blue ink. "Jorge Raminez," he read aloud, writing the case number down on his legal pad. "Yes I have. I know him. We both worked for the City at the same time. Homestead, eh? I wondered what happened to him." Rehnquist paused, trying to think of a way to soften the blow, but couldn't. "To be honest Grace . . . he's a fuck-up. Probably the worst possible choice of detectives to assign to your brother's disappearance. I'm sorry."

"Don't be," she said and smiled. "Best news I've heard in days."

Chapter Eleven

Rehnquist handed the business card back to Grace. She took it, sat back down, and crossed her legs.

"My first impression of Detective Raminez left me feeling that he wasn't overly competent, and if what you say is true—"

"It is."

"—then that gives me even more confidence that you'll be able to find Jason."

Not wanting his expression to betray his own lack of confidence, Rehnquist went back to his legal pad, reviewing his notes from the day before, making the occasional check mark.

Grace continued. "Honestly, I didn't like Raminez as soon as I met him. Not a nice man . . . zero compassion. You could just tell that I interrupted his coffee break. He took my statement and asked a few questions, but the whole time I felt like he was just placating me. But to be honest . . . I guess he didn't have much to go on." Grace frowned and looked off into the distance.

"Grace, the last time you talked with Jason, what did you talk about?"

"Nothing in particular, mostly the old days."

"The old days?"

"The Keys. Fishing. George and Betty."

"Was this unusual?"

"No, we often did. He just seemed to be a bit more reflective than usual . . . pensive, I guess."

"How so?"

"I don't know. At first he sounded fine, but once he started talking about growing up and holidays and vacations spent with George and Betty, he began to sound sad. A week before at dinner he brought up the picture that was taken at George and Betty's house off Tarpon Basin. The first one I showed you at Jake's."

Rehnquist nodded.

"We went to Cape Sable that day. Ever been?"

"Once, with George."

"Then you know. It was probably our most favorite place to visit. George always said 'God lives there.'"

Rehnquist smiled in acknowledgement. He'd heard George say that too.

Grace returned the smile. "First Jason talked about spending the day at Middle Cape. We anchored up and played around on the beach, picking up what few shells we found there, and then we had a picnic, thanks to Miss Betty. We could never get her out on the boat, but Lord knows she always took care of us. I miss those days." Grace's smile broadened. Then Jason talked about getting back to the dock, and George taking that picture. He said, 'You remember that picture.' I said yes, I have a copy in my office, pinned to the wall. He said, 'That's right, I forgot.'"

"Nothing wrong with a little reminiscing," Rehnquist said. "Grace, could I trouble you for a little more coffee?"

"I'm sorry, Nick. I'm not a very good hostess today," Grace said, as she rose to take his cup.

"Nonsense. I'm keeping you occupied. And while you're at it, I need to visit the little boy's room."

"First door on the left. Please excuse the girly mess. I may be Jason's sister, but I still consider myself a visitor here—thus the guest bath."

Once Rehnquist finished his business, he saw what she meant. Nearly every inch of the vanity top was taken, and washing his hands required working around a menagerie of makeup, brushes, curling irons, and a hair dryer. He returned to a full cup of steaming coffee, and Grace continued where she left off.

"Just like at dinner the week before, toward the end of our conversation, Jason brought up Cape Sable again. He said that he wanted to see if George would take us back there again sometime for another picnic. Then, about an hour after we hung up, he sent me a scanned copy of the picture at George's dock—twice. Both times as an attachment to an email that said, 'Hey sis, look what I found. Happy times.'"

"Twice?"

"Yes. The only thing I can think of is that he thought that the first one didn't go through and resent it. I was going to ask him about it later, but . . ." she stopped, and the look of hopelessness returned to her face. "That picture was my last contact with Jason. That's why I brought my copy of it the first night we met." Grace brushed away a tear.

Rehnquist reached over and softly touched her arm. "I'm sorry." He gave her a moment and then asked, "Grace, why would he send a you a copy of that photo, when a week before you reminded him that you had a copy pinned to your office wall?"

"I don't know, it doesn't make any sense, does it?"

"No, it doesn't. Could you please forward those two emails to me? In fact, unless there's something personal or inappropriate that you don't feel comfortable sharing, could you please forward me any emails or text messages between you and Jason over the past six months? Or better still, go back three months before he left the school system."

"Sure. What are you looking for?"

"I don't know," Rehnquist said. He reached into his wallet and pulled out a business card, put an asterisk to the left of his email address, and handed it to Grace. "Maybe something that you might have missed. It could be that you're too close—ignorance can be a very useful tool to an investigator. I might pick up on something you didn't see."

"There won't be many texts Nick. I changed phones a few months ago."

"Do you still have your old phone?"

"Yes, I kept it for a spare."

"Is it an iPhone?"

"Yes."

"Unless you erased them, the text messages will still be on the phone. If you charge it and connect to Wi-Fi, you can forward them to my phone just like your phone was still in service."

"Okay, when I get home I'll do that."

"Did Jason use Facebook or other social media?"

"He used to have a Facebook account, but he deleted it when he applied for the school board job. He was afraid that the wrong person might see something and think it was inappropriate."

Rehnquist nodded. "How about girlfriends? Any recent romantic interests?"

Grace sighed. "I'm clueless on that one. Jason hasn't talked about anyone that he was interested in . . . in forever. He did have two girlfriends that he was close to at one time—well, not girlfriends, *girl* friends—but they haven't heard from him in several weeks. I forgot. I called them. I have their numbers here," she said picking up her phone. "Karen Austin and Julie Danvers." When she read the second name Rehnquist felt an old familiar pain. Grace read off their phone numbers, and Rehnquist wrote them down on his legal pad. "He used to hang out with Karen at college, and Julie is a computer geek that he met more recently at some seminar. A beautiful girl, but he was only interested in her mind." Grace smiled, shrugged, and raised her brow as if to say, what are you gonna do?

"Friends at work? Other friends from college?"

Grace just shrugged.

"What about the neighbors, did they see anything—when did they see him last?"

"The units on both sides are in foreclosure and have been vacant for months. The one on the far end is owned by snowbirds, and they haven't been here since at least April. The other unit is occupied by a thirtysomething radiology tech that works over at the hospital. I spoke with her. She works the evening shift, and couldn't even tell me the last time she saw Jason."

"What about the neighbors down below?"

"Only three units are occupied, and I spoke with each of the residents. None of them could remember seeing anything out of the ordinary, or to seeing Jason after Wednesday, the last night I spoke with him."

Rehnquist glanced back to the legal pad, and referred to his notes. "What about his finances?"

"I'm not sure. He has a small mortgage on the condo, but no other debt that I'm aware of. His car is paid off, and he's pretty frugal. I know he banks and pays his bills online—because he's been after me to do it for years. I'm hip to technology, but I'm still more comfortable writing checks. Thank God his mortgage and utilities are automatic debits; otherwise—"

"We'd be sitting in the dark."

"Literally."

"What about important documents? — Life insurance policies? — A will?

"I've looked through his files here—they're all in a single file drawer in his desk—there's next to nothing. Most of his records are kept electronically, on his computer, or in 'the cloud' as he would say." She looked bewildered. "I use a computer, and I have a smart phone, but whenever Jason would talk about the cloud, I was lost."

"That's okay," Rehnquist said, "remember, I'm reformed. I'm pretty good with a computer and I use cloud storage myself. I also have connections with people who know a lot more about computers and digital storage than I do. So, if Jason has left us anything that will give us a clue as to his whereabouts or what happened to him, we'll find it," he said confidently, as if he actually believed it.

"Good. Thank you," she said, her expression only slightly giving away her sudden lack of confidence. "Jason hated paper, but he may have something at the bank. He has a safe deposit box. Actually I have a key— home of course—and, he has a key to mine . . . I just haven't found the strength to go through it." Grace suddenly realized that she had gone through Jason's belongings at the condo, and hadn't seen keys to either his or her safe deposit box. She continued, "Since neither of us have children, we look out for one another."

"Does he have life insurance?"

"Yes, half a million I think. Mom is the primary beneficiary, I'm the contingent."

"Grace, have you come across his passport?"

"No, I haven't. But he doesn't travel much; I suppose it could be in the safe deposit box."

Rehnquist nodded. "Okay, and what about his computer? Is it here?"

Grace shook her head. "No. Jason only used a laptop—and he had an iPad, and he took them everywhere with him."

"So, neither are here?"

"No."

"I could use a recent picture or two of him; got anything I can use?"

"Sure, just a minute." Grace picked up her phone and began flipping through her photos. "Here's a couple of nice ones. I took these at Black Point Marina one

Sunday a couple of months ago. Want me to text them to you?"

"How about AirDrop?"

"Sure, I always forget about that."

A moment later Rehnquist had both photos. "Thanks. Okay, just a couple more questions. What did Jason drive?"

"A three-year-old blue Miata."

"Any clue as to his license plate number?"

"'J-A-R'."

"Jar?"

"No," she laughed. "J-A-R, Jason Alan Roberts. Plates like mine—only he has a Gator."

"I wondered about your plates. 'DGR'?"

"Dorothy Grace Roberts. I'm named after my father's mother."

"Nice. I like honoring relatives, and I like the initials, but couldn't either of you have chosen better teams?"

Grace delivered a swift swat to his left shoulder. "Hey!"

"Sorry, but you have to admit that you both had pretty tough seasons last year."

Grace just rolled her eyes.

Rehnquist smiled. "Okay, enough football for today. How about one more coffee, and then we'll plan our day?"

"Okay, but what about the *particulars*? I guess we should discuss your fee."

"Grace, we have so little to go on, I'm still not sure what, if anything I can do to find out what happened to Jason—but I'll give it my best. You have me for one week. If I can't find *something, anything,* to go on, it's time to involve law enforcement again—only above the local yokels here. Hopefully we can at least find *something* that might interest the State, or better yet, the Feds. And there *is* no fee, expenses only—"

"Nick, n—"

"Grace, I can't charge for this one. Once I sat down and talked with George, I realized just how much Jason means to him. I saw the pain in his eyes, Jason is the son he always wanted, but never had."

"But—"

"Grace!" Rehnquist cut her off, holding a finger to his lips. "No buts Grace. This is not about money. As he was for Jason, George was there for me at a time in my life when I needed him more than I could ever have imagined. I can never repay him for that—but maybe I can make a difference here. But I sure as hell won't take anyone's money. As I started to say, expenses only—but only if they get out of hand."

"I understand. Thank you." Grace said, as she reached over and clasp his hand.

"Okay, let's forget about the coffee," Rehnquist said. "We'd better get busy. First, we need to check out the contents of the safe deposit box. Any chance you could go home and get the key?"

"Sure. I'll also pick up my old cell phone and charger. If I leave soon, I can be back by about three-thirty."

"That's pushing it for the bank. Go, but drive safe. We can always do it tomorrow. Meanwhile I'm going to follow up with Raminez and see if I can figure out what, if anything he did to locate Jason, and then I have a few other things I want to check out. We'll meet up later."

Chapter Twelve

"Grace was overly optimistic when she had estimated her arrival time back to Homestead. She forgot about the recent construction on the Turnpike, and was delayed just long enough to hit the first round of rush hour traffic. No way could she make it back by the time the bank closed. By now she was anxious to see if anything was in Jason's safe deposit box, so this was just one more thing in a long list of recent disappointments. When reality finally hit her, she picked up her phone.

"Nick . . . I'm sorry. I'm still an hour out."

"Don't worry about it, we'll go to the bank first thing in the morning."

"But I—"

"I know, I'm sorry too. Grace, did you have lunch?"

"No."

"Me neither. I'm starved, how about you?"

Grace took a second to decide if she was up to it. "I could eat."

"Capri?"

"Sure."

"Okay, I'll grab a high top at the bar—if that's alright."

"That's fine. See you in an hour."

Rehnquist was early and was halfway through his first martini by the time Grace arrived. The hostess looked surprised when Grace said no thank you to the offer of a table, that she was meeting a friend at the bar. Maybe the Capri was a bad idea. Too many people knew her here, and she wasn't prepared to answer questions today. Fortunately, even though the hostess was full of questions, she never really waited for answers, but kept right on talking.

"Fine, thank you. No, thank you. I'm meeting someone at the bar. No, the handsome stranger is just a friend. No, you haven't met him before. Yes, he is a nice man. Yes, it's been a while, I'll tell Jason you said hello. Good to see you too." *That wasn't too painful, but I hope that's the last one tonight.*

"Nick, I hope your day was better than mine," Grace said, as she sighed and slumped down in the chair across the table from him.

"I'll let you be the judge." Rehnquist motioned toward the hostess stand, and said, "I'm sorry, I suggested the Capri earlier because I thought it might spur another memory of your last time here. Something you might have forgotten. I had suggested the bar because I thought it might be easier for you. I saw your exchange with the hostess when you arrived. In hind sight I guess we should have gone somewhere else."

"Grace?" the bartender said from across the bar, holding up a wine glass.

"Yes," she nodded. "That's okay Nick. I didn't think about it either—I should have."

"Do you want to just finish our drinks and go somewhere else?"

"No," she said and smiled, patting his hand, "I'll be fine. Really."

"Did you get the safe deposit box key?"

"Yes," she said, as she reached into her purse, "and my old phone, and charger, and something else."

"Some . . . thing . . . else?"

"The safe deposit box key was in a file folder wrapped in this." She handed Rehnquist a copy of a signatory authorization form for two bank accounts for Jason Alan Roberts, listing Dorothy Grace Roberts as an authorized signer. The form was dated October 26, 2001. "I forgot all about these. Jason and I are both authorized signers on each other's checking and savings accounts—assuming these are still valid accounts. We were straight out of school—and it seemed like a good idea at the time."

"Good. This could be helpful. We'll find out tomorrow."

"So Nick, how *was* your day?"

"Well, my first order of business was to call Raminez. I called his office and left a message, then I called a friend at Homestead PD and got his cell number. He didn't answer that either, so I left another message. He called me back a couple of hours later, and agreed to meet me tomorrow at nine o'clock at his office.

"Then I stopped by the personnel department at the school board, and tried to find out who Jason worked for, and with. Of course they were tight-lipped, so I requested Jason's personnel file. I received a definitive 'no,' until I reminded them of their statutory requirement to comply with the state's public records law and provide his redacted records." Rehnquist smiled, "They should be ready for pick up tomorrow morning. Hopefully I can figure out from his evaluations and promotional documents who his supervisors were."

"That's a start . . ."

"Most important, I called a friend who works for the FBI and played the friendship card. He checked with TSA and there is no record of Jason leaving the country using *his* passport by commercial air or ship—although it is relatively easy to fly by private charter to Mexico or the islands under the radar, as long as you land at a private airfield, and don't clear customs. Ditto for water crossings. Oh, my friend also checked domestic flights . . . nothing."

"Is that good or bad," Grace asked.

"I'm not sure," Rehnquist said with a shrug, just as the bartender delivered Grace's Chardonnay. Rehnquist pointed to his empty glass, "I'll have another please, same vodka, only this time dirty, with three olives."

"Coming right up sir," the bartender said. "Menus?"

"Yes please," Grace said, "and two glasses of water."

Rehnquist wanted the prime rib, but it was the wrong night of the week, so he settled for a rare 5 oz. filet instead, with a baked potato. Probably a better choice anyway. Smaller and without all the fat. Still, he was disappointed, he really wanted the prime rib. Grace wasn't surprised when he ordered red meat, but he did throw her for a loop when he washed it down with a Cabernet. Rehnquist watched as Grace slowly picked through her chicken salad. *So that's how she keeps her weight off.* "Your usual, or just not hungry tonight?"

She laughed. "No, sometimes I go all out here, and have soup too. Guess I'm just not all that hungry."

The remainder of dinner was spent in small talk, and when they were finished eating and having coffee, they took a moment to go over their plans for the morning.

"Tomorrow, after I talk to Raminez, and after we go to the bank, I plan on talking with Jason's old coworkers. While I'm doing that, could you work on sending me the texts and emails?

"Sure. As soon as we leave at the bank I'll go back to Jason's and send you what I have. Some of the older emails may be archived on my desktop at home. I'll have to send you those later."

Rehnquist yawned and looked sleepy-eyed at Grace. It had been a long day, and he was tired. "I can't imagine Raminez taking more than half an hour—assuming he's on time. If it looks like we're going to be longer, I'll call you. Otherwise, want to meet at the bank at ten?"

"Sure. It's just off the Turnpike, next exit after Campbell. I'll text you the address. Nick, are you driving back to the Keys tonight?"

"Not after three of these," he said, pointing to his empty Martini glass.

"Three? I only count two."

"Night's not over Grace, nights not over."

Chapter Thirteen

The next morning Grace and Rehnquist were sitting in the lobby at the bank, waiting for the attendant to finish with two customers ahead of them. While they were waiting, Rehnquist filled Grace in on his meeting with Raminez. "What a waste of time—ninety minutes. First, he was nearly forty minutes late, and then he left our meeting four times to take phone calls—the hell of which, at least two of them were from his new wife. I could hear him talking outside the door. All cutesy wootsy. It was nauseating."

Grace just looked dumbfounded.

"I got absolutely nothing out of him, other than he put out a BOLO on Jason and his car, and talked to one of his neighbors. When I asked him for a copy of his report he had the audacity to say that he couldn't do that, that it's still an open investigation. Asshole. And to think we used to work together. What ever happened to professional courtesy?"

Grace glanced down at her watch, and began fidgeting nervously with its band. "Oh, bad news on the bank accounts Nick. I checked before you got here. Both accounts were closed years ago. I explained my situation to the teller, but all she could tell me was that they both were closed. I know that Jason still banks here, because I was with him one day and he drove out of his way to use this ATM so he wouldn't have to pay a transaction fee."

"He may have opened a different type of account—money market or something like that."

Grace nodded in agreement. They sat in silence for the next few minutes, patiently waiting their turn. "I should have done this before now," Grace finally said. "I guess I just blocked it out of my mind. It seems like such an invasion of his privacy—or an admission that he's never coming back." Grace started to tear up.

Rehnquist took her hand. "It is an invasion of his privacy, but we've got no choice. Hopefully we'll find something." Sensing the need for a momentary change of subjects, Rehnquist said, "Grace, I don't even know what you do—I mean for work."

"I'm mostly retired, thanks to my cheating ex-husband, the plastic surgeon. But I also occasionally act as a buyer's agent on high-end real estate sales. In terms of the divorce, he left me well off. There was really little need for attorneys—he wanted a quiet, uncontested divorce; otherwise he felt like it might damage his practice, since most of his patients are women. So, basically he made me an offer—"

Grace suddenly stopped at the approach of a hurried middle-aged woman dressed for success in a black pantsuit, heels clacking on the tile floor. "Hello, I'm sorry for the delay. Please follow me Ms. Roberts."

A few minutes later Grace and Rehnquist were sitting in the viewing area of the vault. Grace nervously raised the lid on the box as Rehnquist looked on. Inside were three large manila envelopes. In the center of the top envelope the word 'PERSONAL' was printed in small block letters. In the same location on the envelope below was 'INS., PROPERTY AND ACCOUNTS.' On the third envelope the word 'NEGATIVES' was printed. Jason was very organized—maybe to the point of being compulsive.

Grace opened the clasp on the first envelope and slid the contents onto the table: Jason's birth certificate, social security card, passport, and copies of his driver's license and health insurance cards paper-clipped to an original living will. Graced gasped when she saw the passport; clearly she wasn't expecting that. Rehnquist put his arm around her and said, "That doesn't mean a thing, other than he isn't traveling, or he isn't traveling with *his* passport. And, we already knew that there was no record of him clearing TSA. There are many other possibilities . . ." Grace nodded, in silence, and slid everything back into the envelope, and went on to the second.

The first items that slid out of the second envelope were a 32 GB USB flash drive and a safe deposit box key. They had been lying atop a piece of paper printed with a list of account names and numbers for checking and savings accounts, an IRA, an annuity, utilities, and several credit card accounts; followed by his life insurance policy, mortgage documents marked paid, and a copy of the deed for his condo. Apparently he had paid off the mortgage. At the bottom of the stack was a copy of his license plate registration for the current year, but no car title.

Rehnquist picked up the key and held it up momentarily. "Key to your safe deposit box?"

"Most likely—but I still haven't found his. It must be well hidden."

"Or, he has it with him."

Grace nodded.

In the final envelope were at least two dozen black and white photographic negatives, and several dozen color. All were cut into strips and preserved in protective plastic sleeves. Rehnquist held one of the sleeves with color negatives up to the light. "Children," he said. "You and Jason?"

Grace took the sleeve from Rehnquist, and looked at it carefully. "Yes, I think so," she said, handing it back to him.

"The black and whites?"

"Most likely my grandparents and my parents right after they were first married," Grace said. "I remember Mom giving these to him about a year ago. He scanned them and then sent us copies. I have them on my computer at home."

With Grace's approval, Rehnquist carefully photographed all of the items from the first envelope and the page with the account names and numbers from the second, making certain that each digital photo was clean, crisp, and legible. Grace held on to the safe deposit box key, and passed the flash drive on to Rehnquist. He lightly squeezed her hand when he took it, acknowledging his responsibility, and the drive's potential importance. "We'll look at these later, together," he said. Grace then made certain that everything went back into the proper envelopes, closed the box and took it back to the attendant.

As they walked back through the bank lobby, Rehnquist said, "I'm off to pick up Jason's personnel file, and we'll see where that leads me. Are you okay?"

"Yes, thank you. I'll be alright. I'll go back and work on the texts and emails. Please let me know if you have any luck."

"You sure? You sure you're alright?"

"I'm sure, Nick," Grace said, and sighed.

"Okay." Rehnquist didn't believe her, but what could he do? He waited until they were outside the bank and away from any potential listeners. "Now that I have Jason's social, I'll pull a credit report and seen if there has been any recent activity on his credit cards."

"Can you do that without his consent?"

"I have a . . . an acquaintance that works at a credit agency. He likes the ponies and likes to spend his weekends up at Gulfstream Park watching them run around in circles. He's always looking for a little cash to advance his hobby, so the short answer is 'yes.'"

Grace shot a bemused look his way. "Didn't you use to be a cop?"

"Yep. Interestingly enough, that's how I met him. His car matched a car that I was looking for, so I pulled him over. When I walked up to the car the smell of pot billowed out the window."

"So you arrested him?"

"Nope. He had like ten grams on him, and he wasn't selling. I was looking for a much bigger player—a coke dealer—so I chewed his ass for driving half-stoned and told him to go home. Hell, I even gave his pot back to him."

"No way."

"Way. When you work vice, sometimes the little things pay off in big dividends later.   Hell, I'm glad I didn't bust him—or a dozen other guys like him. For what? Shit's gonna be legal in a couple years anyway. I was just ahead of my time. A real visionary . . ."

Chapter Fourteen

Grace walked back to her car thinking about what
Rehnquist had just told her. *Now I understand what George
and Betty see in Nick and why they like him. What a trip.
Maybe a little full of himself, but . . .* Despite their age
differences, he's the kind of man she might have wanted
to have met a few years before, instead of the losers she
ended up with. *Better lose that thought.*

She climbed into her car and started it up. As
soon as the radio came on she shut it off. No music
today. Going through Jason's safe deposit box seemed to
take away any hope she had of ever seeing him again. The
drive back to his house was shear hell, and no matter how
hard she tried to fight back the tears, they came. The
sadness and despair grew with every breath and with each
passing mile. When she finally reached Jason's she let go
of her emotions; everything she had been holding back

from the first time he didn't answer her call. She sat in the car in the parking space and cried until she was numb.

Finally, she pulled herself together and went inside. She put her old cell phone on charge, poured a glass of wine and sat down at her computer. Jason didn't send that many emails. Most were jokes or comics that he forwarded from friends and acquaintances that she didn't know. That might be an avenue for Rehnquist to pursue.

Grace knew that she was notoriously bad about cleaning up her emails—even when it came to emptying the deleted items from her trash folder. This was one time she was glad that she was. She hadn't archived anything in over fifteen months, and the deleted items went back for over five months.

When Rehnquist first asked for the emails, she planned to read all of them prior to sending them to him in case there was something that she didn't want him to see. Now that she was actually in the process, she decided to send them all, and to intentionally not read any of them. Other than the fact that she was not emotionally prepared to read them, or the text messages, she couldn't imagine anything too embarrassing in them, and even if there was something, she knew that she could trust him; otherwise, George would never have recommended him.

Starting with her inbox, she began with the earliest email and continued to the last. Then she moved on to sent items, and then finally forwarded a few from trash that she had previously deleted. She completed her task in less than an hour. Next she turned to her phone. Most of the text messages between her and Jason were contained within just a few continuous threads, so it only took a few minutes to send them all.

When she finished forwarding the texts from her new phone, she moved on to the old one. She took it off the charger and connected it to Wi-Fi. Fortunately, she wasn't any more diligent about deleting old texts than she was her emails, and several from Jason dated back to when she first bought the phone, almost three years ago. A few of the texts were three-way conversations that also included an old girlfriend that Grace had never met, when Jason had shot a selfie and sent it to both of them. *Jan or Janet . . . Janet somebody.*

* * *

On his way to the HR department at the school, Rehnquist stopped by to see his acquaintance that loved the ponies. He dropped off an envelope which contained a page from his legal pad with his phone number, Jason's name, social security number and date of birth written on it, and a C-note conspicuously paper clipped to the top of the page. After he left he decided to call and ask a favor from an old friend who still worked at the city. The favor would require a slight breach of departmental policy, but Detective Ansco wouldn't mind—especially once he knew it was to help George. Not long after Rehnquist moved to the Keys, Ansco came down for a day of fishing. George took them out in the backcountry and they ended up at Flamingo. They didn't catch many fish that day, but Ansco was hooked.

"Why Nick Rehnquist, how the hell 've you been?"

"Just fine Danny, how 'bout you?"

"I can't complain. Don't supposed you called to invite me fishing?"

"'fraid not. To be honest, I need a favor—but it does involve George."

Rehnquist told Ansco about his initial meeting with Grace, and how she'd asked him to look into her brother's disappearance following a less than enthusiastic response from Raminez. He then explained her and Jason's connection to George and Betty, and how he'd agreed to look into Jason's disappearance, gratis, as a favor to George.

"I don't know if I can help them or not, but I felt an obligation to my old friend to at least try, especially when I found out who they assigned the case to. When Grace handed me his business card, I tried to think of a way to sugarcoat it, but I couldn't. I told her straight up, he's a fuck-up."

"I understand ol' buddy—you know how I feel about him. We spent way too many years cleaning up his half-assed investigations."

"Yes we did, and I haven't forgotten it."

"Well, after you left, it finally caught up with him and the shit hit the fan."

"What happened?"

"High profile case. He mishandled evidence in the shooting death of a city commissioner's son. The kid was shot outside a convenience store during what was an apparent drug buy. Raminez just assumed he was a dirt bag, and that nobody'd give a shit. Well, somebody did— his parents. By the time they ID'd the body and notified the parents, Raminez had been driving around for two days with the evidence in his back floorboard. Worse yet, the night of the shooting, he didn't even bother to try to find, interview, or even ID two likely eyewitnesses to the whole thing. They had just left the convenience store seconds before the shooting."

"So, how'd he manage to get out of this one?"

"He didn't. He quickly and quietly resigned. I think he wanted to keep his pension. They reassigned the case, but it didn't matter. They were never able to locate the witnesses—and as for the evidence? Half of it wasn't properly labeled, and it was mixed among other poorly marked evidence collected early that day. And, even if the lab had found something—no chain of custody. The shooter's still out there, somewhere."

"Christ. What the hell's he doing working for Homestead?"

"His uncle was a captain there when they hired him."

"Unbelievable. Some things never change."

"See what you miss Nick, living down in the Keys."

"I'm missing nothing but headaches."

"Alright then, enough about Raminez. What can I do to help?"

"Raminez put out a BOLO on Jason and his car, but if I could get you to run his plate, and once you get the VIN on his car, run it and see if you get a hit. Oh, and while you're at it, please run Jason. I'd hate to be looking for him if he's somewhere in Jail."

Ansco asked Rehnquist to text him Jason's full name, date of birth, social security number, and license plate number, and promised to get on it as soon as he got back to his office. Rehnquist thanked him and hung up, and as soon as he pulled into the school administration parking lot, he texted all of Jason's information to him.

As Rehnquist walked toward the administration building, he thought about yesterday's reception. *Today should be interesting.* This was one part of the business that he loved; the way that different people react when you hit them up for information. Most times you could sweet talk your way into what you needed—often all you had to do was ask. Some people were almost giddy when it came to telling on coworkers, friends, and neighbors. Just a little gossip. Letting someone else in on a little secret. Sometimes it took more; you had to dole out a little cash. It never ceased to amaze him how many people would sell out their own mother for a few dollars.

Bureaucrats and other disinterested public employees required a different approach. They were often reluctant, even unwilling to help; quick to say, 'no, I can't do that.' But Rehnquist learned a long time ago that one of his best tools in obtaining information was Florida's liberal public records law. With it you could obtain just about anything, including the personnel records of virtually every city, county, and state employee with rare exceptions, and even most of those had to be provided on demand with a handful of redactions.

Today, he only had to deal with a run-of-the-mill public employee, Maggie, the lady with the attitude who had waited on him yesterday. He couldn't really blame her for her attitude. It was one thing to spread a little water cooler gossip, but a request for records required actual work, a distraction from the normal work of the day. He walked into the administration building and went into the HR department. Maggie immediately recognized him, and promptly handed him a sealed manila envelope and a bill for $3.45; 23 pages at $.15 per page for photocopying. Rehnquist thanked her and summarily dropped four, one dollar bills on the counter.

"I don't have change," she grumbled.

Rehnquist just shrugged and said, "Sorry, I don't either, and I also don't have a check. Donate it to the scholarship fund," as he turned and walked out. Once he climbed into his car and opened the envelope he realized that he might have left the HR department prematurely. *Shit, three supervisor names and not a clue as to where to find them. Hopefully I can get their phone numbers from the online school directory.*

Rehnquist crossed his fingers and took out his phone. He was lucky. The phone directory was mobile friendly, and two of the three supervisors were listed. He called them both, and neither had seen or spoken with Jason since he left the school system. They both sang his praises, and said that they were surprised and disappointed to see him go. They also told him that the other supervisor, Jason's first, when he began his employment, had moved to Colorado two years ago, and they didn't have any contact information for him.

Rehnquist's next stop was the management office at Jason's condominium, to see what, if anything, was available in security recordings. He was pleased to find out that they maintained thirty days of recordings, and after some swift talking he convinced the manager to let him look at the recordings of the main gate. The gate cameras were motion activated, and captured cars entering and leaving the complex.

He began with the footage from the exit camera, beginning with the previous day and worked his way backwards. Since he was specifically looking for a blue car—which would stand out among the many white and gray cars that passed through the gate each day—he was able to quickly scan through each day using fast-reverse. Soon after he finished his review of the first week and started on the second, his phone rang.

"Rehnquist."

"Nick, it's Danny. I've got news, but you're not gonna like it."

"What is it?"

"Okay, first the BOLO is still out for Jason, and for his car—at least his plates—but I know where to find his car."

"Where?"

"He sold it," Ansco said.

"No fuckin' way."

"He sold it to a used car dealer in Homestead on August 24th. One of those buy here, pay here places."

"Holy shit."

"When I ran the VIN it came back to a Jamal Nixon with a Naranja address. He works at one of the boat yards up on the river. Apparently he bought the car from the dealer the day after Jason sold it. I'm gonna meet the salesman in an hour. You wanna tag along?"

"Sure."

"Regent Auto. Place is just west of South Dixie off Campbell."

"Okay, thanks. See you there."

Rehnquist couldn't imagine why Jason would sell his car. *That won't go over well with Grace.* He went back to the security recordings, and there it was, a blue Miata leaving on August 24th at 10:32 a.m. Switching to the footage of the cars entering the complex, the Miata entered the evening before at 6:23 p.m. In all, the Miata left once or twice each day of the week preceding the 24th. As best he could tell from the camera angle, every time the car was only occupied by the driver, a blond, white male that appeared to be Jason. Rehnquist ran the entrance footage forward after the 24th, and then re-checked the exit footage. There was no sign of the Miata in either.

* * *

Rehnquist pulled into the auto brokers just a few minutes behind Ansco, who was sitting in his car, talking on the phone. Once Ansco saw him, he hung up, got out, and they shook hands. After a few minutes of pleasantries and a little personal catch-up, they went into the sales office in search of answers.

The well-lit building had the feel of a converted 7-Eleven, with a receptionist's desk up front, and several small gray cubicles organized into workstations clustered in the center of the main room. When they walked in, a perky, young brunette looked up from the receptionist's desk, smiled, and said, "Hi, I'm Maria. Can I help you gentlemen?"

"We're here to see Mr. Reynolds—he's expecting us. I'm Detective Ansco, and this is Detective Rehnquist."

"Sure, right this way," she said, as she stood and motioned for them to follow. She ushered them to a small corner office with interior windows facing the front entrance, where Jimmy "Spunk" Reynolds, was sitting at his desk and was just finishing his lunch. Ansco and Rehnquist introduced themselves and shook Reynold's hand.

"Thank you for agreeing to see us on such short notice," Ansco said.

"No problem, it's a slow day anyway," Reynolds said, as he collected his sandwich wrapper and tossed it into the trash. "Please, have a seat," he said, gesturing toward two metal framed plastic chairs.

Ansco and Rehnquist sat down, and Ansco asked, "So what can you tell us about Mr. Roberts and his car?"

"Well, he came in here on a Friday—what was it, the twenty-first, I think—and asked if we'd be interested in buying his car. I was busy with another customer, so I asked him to have a seat and told him I'd be with him shortly. When I finished, I told him our preference is to sell used cars on commission—which gives him a better price—and then we charge a percentage of the sales price."

"What'd he say?" Ansco asked.

"He said he was in a hurry to sell. Something about needing the money, and he couldn't afford to wait for a buyer to come along. I looked over the car, and had my mechanic check it out. It was clean and in good shape, so I offered him thirteen-eight. That's a steep discount off the average market price, but hell, you never know how long a car might sit on the lot. He said he'd think about it, and then he came back on Monday, and accepted my offer. An hour later he cleaned out the car and left with his license plate and a cashier's check for fourteen even—I felt sorry for the kid so I threw in a couple extra."

Ansco and Rehnquist looked at each other. The car was in inventory for less than a whole day. Reynolds was not just a used car salesman; he was a regular fucking philanthropist.

"I offered him a ride," Reynolds said, "but he said, no thanks, he'd use Uber."

Rehnquist took out his phone and showed Reynolds Jason's picture, and asked him to confirm that he was the man who had brought the car in. Reynolds said that he was, and then he pulled the file on the transaction and attached to the bill of sale was a copy of Jason's driver's license.

"Gentlemen, what's this about, anyway? The car wasn't used in a crime or something, was it?"

"No, Mr. Reynolds, the car is just fine," Rehnquist said. "We're just following up on Mr. Robert's whereabouts over the past couple of weeks—that's all."

As they were leaving, Ansco turned back to Reynolds and said, "You said he cleaned out his car. I would've thought he would've already done that before he came in."

"Yeah, me too—most people do. But for whatever reason he didn't. But it only took him a minute. Basically he just popped the trunk and took out a couple of small suitcases and a backpack—like he had some place to go. The glovebox, seats, everything else was already cleaned out."

* * *

On his way back to meet Grace, Rehnquist stopped off at the credit agency and picked up Jason's credit report. Three pages, paper clipped together, but he didn't look at it; he waited until he was back at Jason's house to share it with Grace. "Well, his credit cards are all paid off, and apparently no activity on any of them for months," Rehnquist said.

"What about his checking or savings accounts?"

"Sorry, those aren't included in credit reports."

"Oh," Grace said, in disappointment.

Rehnquist brought her up-to-date on his conversations with Jason's supervisors: Excellent employee and a spotless record, and they both were surprised when he abruptly turned in his two-weeks' notice. Then he told her about reviewing the security footage, and finally, saving the worst for last, about Jason's last trip through the gate confirmed by the sale of his car. She was devastated.

"He sold his car?"

"Yes."

"I don't believe it."

"I'm sorry Grace. He sold it—to an auto broker who's already resold it.

"Why?"

"He told the broker that he was in a hurry and needed the money. Obviously that's not true—at least not the part about needing the money. He did after all, payoff his mortgage and his car, and he's debt free. But I do believe that he was in a hurry to get rid of it.

"But why?"

Rehnquist just shrugged and shook his head.

Chapter Fifteen

Rehnquist pulled Jason's flash drive out of his pocket, held it up between his thumb and index finger, and waved it back and forth. "Are you up to seeing what's on this?"

Grace nodded. "Sure. I can't imagine the day getting any worse."

"Okay," Rehnquist said, as he opened his laptop and pressed the power button.

Grace stood up and began walking toward the kitchen. "Cocktail?" she called over her shoulder.

"Sure, what does Jason have?"

"Rum, vodka, gin, a little of everything—except beer."

"Great. How about vodka?"

"Vodka it is. Grey Goose—on the rocks?"

"Yes please—but light on the ice."

Grace poured his drink while Rehnquist plugged in the flash drive. By the time she returned, he had the single folder on the drive open on his computer.

"Pictures?" she asked, handing him his drink.

"Not just pictures, pictures of all of his stuff." There were room and contents photos taken throughout the condo. Multiple angles of every room, of electronics and furnishings, pictures inside closets and inside every drawer and cabinet. Inventory lists with serial numbers, and receipts for the big screen TV, computer, iPhone, iPad, furniture, the everglades painting, a bracelet, ring, and three watches. "This drive and his safe deposit box is his hurricane safety kit. No revelations here."

Grace sighed.

Rehnquist ejected the USB drive, pulled it out of his computer and handed it to Grace. Looking down at the screen he said, "Damn updates," and hit restart. While his computer rebooted, he glanced at his phone and the email folder. "Wow, you've been busy."

"I had more emails and messages than I thought. I'm glad Jason convinced me to keep my old phone. I wanted to donate it to some . . . worthwhile cause, but he said I should keep it as a spare, in case I lost or broke my new one, I could use it until I got it fixed, or got a replacement."

"Good advice," Rehnquist said, and then looked up suddenly. "Grace, what about Jason, does he have any old phones?"

"He has an old iPhone in his desk drawer. I saw it the other day."

"Please, go get it."

Two minutes later Rehnquist was plugging Jason's old iPhone 5 into its charger, and waiting for it to boot. While Grace freshened up his Grey Goose and poured herself a glass of Chardonnay, Rehnquist said, "This is probably hopeless; we'll never guess his password."

When Grace brought Rehnquist his drink, he was staring perplexed at the phone. She sat his drink down on the end table beside him, and asked, "What is it?"

He held up the phone up to show her. On the display, centered in large letters on what should have been the lock screen, was 'Hello,' and at the bottom, 'slide to setup.'

"It's wiped clean."

"What do you mean?"

"He reset it to factory settings—like a brand new phone. He erased all his data, apps and all."

"Why would he do that?"

"I don't know. Normally if you keep a phone for backup, you leave it as it is, so you can quickly put it back in service—like your phone. You wouldn't reset it unless you are selling it, trading it in on a new one, or you intentionally want to erase everything on the phone . . ."

Chapter Sixteen

The next morning Rehnquist had the pleasure of waking up in his own bed. After a long day of dead ends and disappointments, he was ready to head back to the Keys. When he left Jason's, Grace really looked exhausted and distraught. He felt bad, but there wasn't anything that he could say that would make a difference. The day had been that bad. He was anxious to start going through the emails and text messages—hoping he could find something there—but he wanted to wait until he was fresh. So, he told Grace goodnight and drove back home for what he hoped would be a decent night's sleep.

When he arrived home, Hope greeted him at the top of the stairs, and was very happy when he set out food and fresh water. Rehnquist took a few moments and sat down on the top step beside her, keeping her company while she ate. When she was finished he gave her a good scratch under her chin, and then went inside.

He plugged the laptop into its charger, popped the top on an Octoberfest, and sat down in the recliner with his iPad.

Since the emails were right there in his mailbox, he was tempted to skim over them, but he resisted, and chose instead to unwind with an e-book, a techno-thriller that he had started weeks ago. A half-dozen pages later, he was fast asleep. Within the hour, he awoke in a cold sweat with a racing heart, and sat bolt upright, knocking the iPad to the floor. Even though he was exhausted, still the nightmare came, and with it the all of the guilt and anxiety. He did his best to shake it off, got up, picked up his iPad and tossed it into the chair. He hoped that the worst was behind him, shut off the light, and went to bed. Fortunately for him it was, and he awoke the next morning to the sound of his alarm, reasonably refreshed and ready for a run.

Five miles later, after a quick shower, his first cup of coffee and a protein bar, he started reading Jason's emails. He read every one carefully, aloud, reading for content and looking for anything that might be concealed within the text. Then he took note of the email address from the original if it was forwarded, or if Jason sent it to anyone other than Grace, those addresses as well. He recorded each address the first time that he saw it on the page of a legal pad that he had divided into two columns: one for senders, the other for recipients. Then, every time the address appeared again, he made a hash mark beside his entry. Later he would check with Grace to see if she knew who the addresses belonged to. Occasionally one contained a first name at the end of a short comment on the original of a forwarded email, so he was able to match Jan, Mark, and Geoff to their addresses—whoever they were. Another question for Grace.

After he finished reading the emails, he moved them into one of several folders that he had created to sort them by topic. Most were cartoons, jokes or links to internet pages. Many contained forwarded material that most people would have shared on social media—if they had an account. Several were short emails that Jason had written to Grace, often late at night when it was too late to call, and after he had remembered something that he wanted to tell her. Many of these were anecdotes about their mother, and some crazy thing she did that week. Rehnquist put these aside for additional scrutiny.

A handful of the emails contained photos, either as attachments, or inserted into the body of the email itself. Most of these were fairly unremarkable—at least at first glance—other than a few of them were also addressed to a second or third recipient. He'd check on those later.

Toward the end he found the email to which Jason had attached the scanned imagines from the black and white negatives he and Grace had seen in the vault, and a second one that mentioned the photos. He also put those aside, and moved onto the final two emails: the ones with the attached photo taken dockside at George's house—the one that Jason had sent twice. He opened both emails, and copied and pasted each photo into its own separate folder, so that it would retain the names, and not add '-Copy' at the end of one of them.

He had a gut feeling about these. It was probably the timing of when they were sent, or Jason forgetting that Grace already had a print of the photo, or that they had discussed it a week before. That, and he still couldn't figure out why Jason had sent them twice, within seconds of one another. Surely if he thought they didn't go through, he would have checked his outbox. He is after all, an IT professional. Then again, maybe it was just a software glitch, a digital hiccup.

Rehnquist got up, stretched his legs, and made another cup of coffee. He sat back down after a few minutes and opened both photos, and compared them side-by-side. They looked exactly the same. Next he tried opening each in Photoshop. He tried multiple enhancements and modifications of each, looked for layers, and he stretched each to an enormous size hoping to see some underlying message or clue. Nothing. So, he gave it a break and went back to the few emails he'd set side.

He opened the one with the black and whites. It had four attached jpg files, along with a message from Jason which read, 'I started scanning the negatives that Mom gave me. Some of these are pretty cool, but the negatives are really faded, and they all have to be touched up. I'll send you the rest when I get finished with them. Love you, J.'

Rehnquist opened up Jason's follow-up email for the photos, which he had placed in the folder with the first. It was sent a week later, under the subject 'Dinner.' There were no photos attached to the email, but the message read, 'Thanks for dinner last night. I had fun but drank too much wine! LOL Here's the link to the rest of the black and whites—enjoy! Love, J.' Below the message was a link to a shared Syncquest folder, with instructions to click the link and enter the login details which included Grace's email address, and an auto generated password, which was given in the email.

Rehnquist clicked the link. It opened a browser window to a login page. He entered Grace's email address and the password and clicked 'Sign In.' A couple of seconds later, a page opened titled 'Jason's Shared Files," Rehnquist clicked the folder and it opened to display some three dozen images.

Chapter Seventeen

For a moment Rehnquist's pulse quickened, thinking that maybe they finally had a break. Jason's Syncquest account was still active. Then it hit him. Of course it was, why wouldn't it be? Even if the worst had happened to Jason, his account would be active until it expired, perhaps at least a year out—or even longer, if he was set up with an automatic renewal on a credit card.

If only he knew Jason's password. He could login to his account and have access to all his files. This would be more than just shared files. It would most likely contain backups of his entire computer. Given Jason's choice of professions, there was little chance of figuring out his password.

Rehnquist was beginning to feel the hint of a headache from eyestrain. Picking up his phone, he checked the time—no wonder, it was almost half past noon. Time to take a break, and time for lunch. Since the refrigerator was still empty he drove up to the deli to pick up a sub, and on his way home, he stopped at the convenience store and bought two six packs of Stella.

Back home, he put the beer in the refrigerator and opened one of the few remaining Octoberfest. Then he woke up the hibernated laptop, moved it over to the kitchen table, unwrapped the sub, and sat down for a working lunch. He downloaded and saved the black and whites from the Syncquest folder to a folder on his desktop, then copied and pasted the four that were attached to the email into their own folder. He'd look at those later. Then he composed an email to Grace.

He listed the email addresses of the people from Jason's forwarded emails and the ones which Jason had cc'd in his emails to Grace. He asked her if she knew who they might belong to, or if she had any idea who Jan, Mark, or Geoff were. Then he picked up his phone and started reading the text messages. An hour later, nothing. All he had to show for his effort was a dead battery. He plugged in his phone, grabbed a Stella, and went back to his laptop and the duplicate photos that Jason had emailed.

Rehnquist right-clicked the first image and opened the details tag in the file properties. Most of the property values were empty with the exception of those typical of scanned photos or documents: file name and type, creation and modification dates, image dimensions and resolutions. There was one property that he didn't recall ever having seen on a scanned image. Under 'Advanced photo,' was a value for 'Camera serial number: 052314-021-007-018-000-009-004-011-016-024-011.' He opened the file folder for his personal photos on his computer and opened the properties for one of his scanned photos. The Camera serial number was empty. He looked at several others, they were empty too. On the final photo, he clicked within the Camera serial number field, which opened a textbox which could be modified by the user. *Jason added those numbers.*

He closed his photos, reopened the properties on Jason's first photograph, and then opened the properties on the second. All properties of the second matched that of the first, with the exception of 'Camera serial number: 052314-002-021-031-036-006-019-000-029-013-007,' which wasn't even close with the exception of the first six digits. Bingo. Up until now, both emails appeared to have as an attachment, the exact, same photo. Clearly it was not the same—or if it was, Jason had at least modified the properties of each, adding a value which would not normally be present. Obviously Jason did not unintentionally send the email twice. He intentionally sent two different versions. But why, and what did the numbers mean?

Rehnquist copied both series of numbers, one above the other, to a Word document and printed them out. As he thought about what they could possibly mean, his phone rang, and he looked at it, bewildered. A number he didn't recognize. "Nick Rehnquist," he answered.

"Hey Nick, Danny Ansco." *Must be his office number.*

"Hi Danny, what's up?"

"What do you know about Uber?"

"Not much, don't need to. Remember where I live. Can you imagine Uber drivers in the Keys? The taxi drivers are scary enough. I can just see calling an Uber driver and having him show up to pick me up after he's had a half dozen beers."

"That's just it Nick, you don't call Uber drivers, there's an app for that. You use the app to submit a trip request, which is then routed to the closest driver."

"So?"

"Okay, say you hail a cab or even call one, what kind of records do they keep? Plus, part of the time they're probably running off the meter—a little side money, save a bit on the taxes. No records right? With Uber, every trip request goes through a server, and the driver picks up that request through his app. When the trip is over, money is exchanged via the app. The client's PayPal account or credit card is charged, and now there is a record of the trip request, point of pick up, and the drop off point. Capisce?

"Got it."

"I don't know why, but that didn't register when we were at the car lot. Then later, I was mulling Jason's situation around in my head, and I remembered that I could put in a law enforcement request and obtain a record of his pick-up."

"Really?"

"Normally they require a subpoena, but they will make exceptions for emergencies. Since Jason's a missing person, and time is of the essence, they made one here. Well, my request just came back. Jason was picked up at 2:16 p.m., at the car dealer's . . ."

"And?"

"He was dropped off forty minutes later, downtown Miami at the Hilton. Then yesterday morning he used the Uber app again, and made a request for a pick up at the hotel with a drop-off at MIA. I checked the hotel records and he checked out yesterday morning. He had a handful of room charges, a couple of trips to the restaurant, bar, and room service. None were too expensive; he must have been by himself. They gave me a copy of the bill; I'll send it to you. Also, his Uber account is on a prepaid Visa card—the same one he used for the hotel."

"Guess he didn't want to use one of his many credit cards."

"Flying under the radar Nick. Now, here's the kicker. I checked with TSA again. Jason was not on any of the flights out of Miami yesterday, and he's not ticketed for today."

"So why the airport?"

"Fake ID? Flying as someone else is my guess, or, he planned on buying a ticket at the airport and suddenly changed his mind."

"Wouldn't he have contacted Uber again for a ride?"

"Maybe not at the airport. Remember, they have an endless line of cabs."

"True."

"Oh, one last thing, I checked his phone records—I did a carrier trace. The last call he made was the one to Grace on the 26th, and then the carrier signal dropped right about the time he made the Uber request at the car dealer."

"How did he use Uber the second time?"

"Probably on Wi-Fi, with the cellular off. Clearly he wants to be off the grid."

"Can't be good."

"I'm sure he's fine, just trying hard not to be found."

"You're a fucking optimist."

"I try. I'll let you know if I find out anything else."

"Danny, thank you. This is way above—"

"Don't mention it."

"No, really, I appreciate it, and I know Grace will too. I'm not sure what any of this means, other than Jason was alive—and hopefully well—in Miami yesterday." Rehnquist hung up the phone and opened his calendar. Day five. His week was almost up, but he wasn't ready to quit. Things were just beginning to look up. They still hadn't found Jason, but at least he found encouragement in Ansco's news. Time to call Grace.

"Grace, I need to talk to you, and I'd like to show you something. Any chance we could meet up tonight?'

"Sorry, I'm meeting a client for dinner at six thirty."

"How about after that?"

"I should be finished and back to Homestead by nine, but that's pretty late for you isn't it, driving up from the Keys?"

"No, I don't mind a late evening. Besides, I was planning on driving up early tomorrow anyway. I'll just spend the night and get an early start tomorrow.

"Okay, want to meet at Jason's?"

Rehnquist thought about it for a second, *Probably not a good idea.* "How about Jake's?"

"Sure, maybe we'll see Robin."

"Yeah, that'd be nice. In any case, if John's working, I know we'll get a good drink."

"Um, maybe too good."

"No, don't say that!"

"Alright Nick, never again. I promise." She said, laughing.

"Okay, that's better. See you tonight."

Rehnquist went back to the two images and the numbers. After thirty minutes he decided to call it quits, and packed his bag for the overnighter. Then he sat out some food and fresh water for Hope and loaded up his car. On his way to the city he decided to stop and check on George and Betty. That turned into a cocktail with George under the chickee, an update on his progress, and what he learned from Ansco earlier.

"I don't know whether to feel good or bad about this," George said.

"My sentiments exactly. But at least we know where he was yesterday morning. That's something."

George agreed. Rehnquist took a sip of his rum and Diet Coke, and then reached into his back pocket and pulled out the printout of the numbers from Jason's photos. He unfolded it and handed it to George. "Any idea what this could mean?"

"What is it?"

"I don't know." Rehnquist told him where the numbers came from. Now the problem was figuring out what they meant.

"Not a clue Nick."

"I didn't think you would, but I was hoping."

Chapter Eighteen

Rehnquist took one last look at the now auburn sky—sun having finished its work for another day, retreating from the approaching storm to the east. For a moment he stood in awe of its beauty, then turned back to watch the distant flash of lightning against the darkening sky. He patiently waited to hear the low rumble of thunder, then stepped into the bar. He was pleased to see that it was almost empty, and that John was tending bar.

He checked with the hostess to see if Robyn was working. She was off, so he sat down at the bar, halfway between the only TV and the cash register, where he figured he could at least interrupt John's attention to the game long enough to get a drink. He hadn't noticed the first time he was here, but the TV was at least twenty years old; a relic in what was otherwise a fairly modern bar. Jake's was certainly not a sports bar. Apparently the owner thought that the couple of hundred dollars it cost to buy a new flat panel could be better spent somewhere else, which was fine with Rehnquist. The only thing he liked about sports bars were the servers' uniforms and the wings.

As soon as Rehnquist sat down, John came over to greet him. "Back again, eh? What can I get you today?"

"Hi John. I'll have a Heineken." *I'm way early, I'd better pace myself.* He reached into his back pocket and pulled out the printout of the photo properties. Unfolding it, he stared at it for several minutes. *What the hell does this mean?* He shook his head, folded it back up and put it back in his pocket. *Tomorrow. I'll worry about it tomorrow.* For a while, he fiddled with his phone, then sat it aside. Then, for the next hour and a half, he sat in quiet contemplation. He thought about his life and the years that had passed since he lost her. Wondering if, when it was all over, did any of it really matter. He was three beers down when Grace interrupted his introspection and returned him to reality.

"Hello Nick."

"Hey Grace." He stood and they exchanged a quick hug. "Get into any rain?" he asked, returning to his seat.

"No, but it looks like it's getting ready to cut loose." she said, sitting down beside him.

"So, how was dinner?"

"Fine thanks, but most likely a waste of time. Guy's looking to buy a big house in Miami near the water, but I think I gave him sticker shock," she said, and laughed.

"Guess it's like a menu without prices at an expensive restaurant. If you have to ask the prices . . ."

"You can't afford it," she completed.

Rehnquist wasn't aware of it, but he was hanging on her every word. During the occasions of their previous meetings, he did his best not to notice just how attractive she was, but tonight, there was no avoiding it, and the chemistry was palpable. She was dressed in a pair of skintight, faded blue jeans, and a tight, white, Cashmere sweater. Her hair hung loose on her shoulders, and she seemed totally relaxed, and carefree.

They sat quietly for a moment, and when Grace broke the silence, Rehnquist realized that he had been staring at her.

"So, what's up?"

"Well for starters, I have some encouraging news."

"Really," she said.

"Yes. Well it's promising at least—"

"Hello again Grace. Chardonnay?" John interrupted.

"Please," she answered. *Wow, he's good, he didn't even wait on me last time. Must have asked Robyn.* Grace turned and looked around the bar. "Guess Robyn's off tonight?"

"Yep, that's why I'm at the bar. Care to join me?"

"Funny, I think I already did."

"Okay, if you say so," Rehnquist said with a wink.

John opened a new bottle of wine, polished a glass and gave Grace a generous pour. "Drink any reds?"

"Occasionally, but usually I stick with whites. I like my wines like my men . . . sweet," she quipped. Rehnquist looked up at John and rolled his eyes. For a second, John looked almost embarrassed. In any case, he kept whatever he was thinking to himself. "Oh, and a water please," Grace said, "need to stay hydrated." John sat a tall glass of ice water in front of her and went back to the game.

Rehnquist started to speak, stopped for a moment and then continued, "Grace, I'm sorry, I never asked. How is your mother handling all this?"

"Oh she's fine. In fact, she's almost happy."

"Happy?"

"Giddy. She thinks Jason's been raptured. She's happy for him."

"Raptured?"

"Yes. Remember what I told you about her and religion? She's convinced that he's been raptured up to heaven."

"Good God." Rehnquist shrugged and looked befuddled. *Looney tunes, time to change topics.* "Okay, here's the good news. My friend, Danny Ansco, the detective that found out that Jason had sold his car, looked into Jason's cell phone records. He also checked into his Uber account. After Jason sold his car, he was picked up at the car dealer by an Uber driver and taken to a hotel in downtown Miami—the Hilton. He stayed there until yesterday morning, when he checked out." He conveniently failed to mention where he went when he was picked up.

Grace sat speechless, trying to absorb what Rehnquist had just told her, unsure if it was good or bad.

Rehnquist placed his hand on her shoulder. "So we know he was in downtown Miami at least up until yesterday. We have to assume he's okay, we just don't know where.   I'm sorry, it's not a lot, but it's a whole lot more than we had."

Rehnquist caught John's attention and ordered a Beefeater tonic.   John nodded in acknowledgment, and looked to Grace, who shook her head.

"You're right, thank you."   She thought about it for a second and said, "So he's been using his phone? Then why doesn't he answer?   Why does it go to voicemail?"

"He hasn't made any phone calls since the last one to you, and the carrier signal has been off, so the phone's been off.   Ansco said that he probably only turned it on to use his Uber app—on Wi-Fi."

"So he really doesn't want to be contacted."

"At least for a time . . ."   He drained the last of his beer and stared absentmindedly at the label.   "Grace, I could have told you that on the phone, but what I really wanted to talk to you about, was . . . well, when I agreed to do this, I said that you had me for one week."   He paused as he set down his bottle, and pushed it back toward John.   "Well, we're five days in, with only two to go."

"What are you saying?"

He turned to face her. "I guess what I'm saying is, I'm not ready to concede defeat. I think we're close. Give me a couple more days."

"Absolutely," she said, and sighed with relief.

"I wanted to give you some positive news about Jason. I hope this helps."

"It does, thank you." She leaned in and put her arm around him and gave him a hug.

John brought Rehnquist his drink and quickly returned to the game. Final few seconds and the score was tied, somebody shooting a free throw. "Shit," John yelped, "there goes twenty bucks." Then he snatched the remote and abruptly flipped the channel to another game—more basketball.

Rehnquist looked at Grace and winked. After a moment he said, "I also need help with this." He pulled out the printout, unfolded it, and spread it out on the bar. Ring any bells?"

"What is it?" she asked, picking it up. While she studied the numbers, Rehnquist told her where they came from, and how he pulled them from the two photos that Jason had sent her. She handed him back the printout, and shook her head. "So he intentionally sent the photo twice?"

"Or at least what appears to be the same photo," Rehnquist said. "Now all we have to do is figure out what these numbers mean, and why he sent them to you."

"So, where do we go from here?"

"I'm not sure, that's why I want more time. That, and the fact that we know that Jason was recently in the area greatly increases the odds of finding him. Our haystack just got a whole lot smaller." Rehnquist sipped his drink and studied the numbers, while Grace slowly watched her wine disappear. After several minutes Rehnquist folded up the printout and put it back in his pocket. Raising his brow, he said, "Sorry, this is driving me crazy."

Grace smiled, "Don't apologize. You're on the clock, even if I'm not paying you."

Rehnquist could feel the gin begin to kick in. "Okay, enough about me. So really, how *was* dinner? Was this a date?"

Grace slapped him on the shoulder. "Nick Rehnquist! I told you what it was. And dinner was just fine thank you, but the next one will be better, now that I know that Jason is alright." Grace picked up her wine and swirled it, watching the tears slowly fall back down the sides of the bowl. "Boy, he really pisses me off. Why would he do this to me?"

"We'll find out—hopefully soon—but I don't think it's about you."

Grace thought about it for a minute. "Yeah, I guess you're right. I hope he's okay." For a moment she almost looked frightened.

"Another round?" John to the rescue.

"Please," Grace said.

"Cosmo for me!"

"Cosmo? That's new. Nick, you are a man of surprises."

"Thanks John, I'll accept that as a complement."

John stepped closer, out of earshot of the other customers at the bar. "I'm actually happy to be a bartender for a change. I get tired of just twisting off beer caps, and you are a virtual Mr. Boston's when it comes to bar patrons."

Rehnquist gave John a quick salute, and said, "That's what I'm here for."

John returned a silly two-finger salute, and headed for his shaker.

"Nick, you seem happy tonight." Grace said.

"I guess I am. Giddy—like your Mom—but for a better reason," he said, pointing to his glass.

"Earlier, when you called and asked about meeting me, you said you were planning on driving up early tomorrow anyway, what's that about?"

"Another trip to the school, that's all."

"Anything in particular?"

"I'm not sure. We'll see."

Rehnquist took the last sip of his gin, and folded his hands on the bar in front of him.

"Nick, you know you don't have to stay in a hotel, Jason has plenty of room. I can stay in his room, and you can have the guestroom—unless that would make you or your wife uncomfortable," Grace said, tapping her left ring finger,

Rehnquist turned to her and looked deep into her blue eyes. Giddiness gone, his eyes lost their splendor, and showed the sadness of a thousand tears. "Grace, my wife is dead."

Chapter Nineteen

"Oh My God! I'm sorry," Grace said, quickly drawing back her hands. "But you have on a wedding band—"

"It's okay," Rehnquist said softly, taking her hand. "I said my wife is dead, I didn't say I'm not married." He paused and took a long look into her eyes. "When I married Julie, and it came time for the vows, when the minister said 'til death do you part,' I interrupted with 'forever.' I can still hear her laugh. I meant it," he said, smiling, as he held up his left hand, and looked down at his wedding band."

"George didn't tell me."

"No, of course he didn't—he wouldn't. He knows how intensely personal this is for me."

"I'm so sorry . . ."

"Grace, my wife was killed. All because of a lottery ticket. A fucking lottery ticket." Rehnquist turned his face away from her, toward the bar, and stared off into the flickering neon of an old beer sign. Grace had never felt more uncomfortable, or more wishing that the floor would cave-in and swallow her up into some alternate reality. John broke the ice when he delivered the round of drinks.

Rehnquist nodded his appreciation to John, took a sip of his Cosmo, and keeping his voice low, turned back to Grace. "Julie loved playing the lottery. Every week, for years, it was the same damn numbers. When she first started, I said, don't choose the numbers, go for a random pick. If you choose the numbers, and you ever forget to buy a ticket, if your numbers are drawn, you'll hate yourself forever. She just laughed, and said that will never happen. Well it did happen. One Sunday morning Julie and I were in bed—sleeping in—and she leapt out of bed with a yelp, and ran into the living room. I jumped up and ran after her and said, what the hell is the matter? By then she was on her computer and thrashing at the keys. She said, 'We forgot to buy a lottery ticket!' I said, so?"

"Julie freaked—at least until she checked the numbers and realized that we hadn't won, or lost—whatever. After that, she swore that we'd never forget to buy a lottery ticket again—and we didn't. When we traveled, she'd buy them in advance; two at a time—sometimes six or eight—week after week."

Grace shifted her position on her stool and leaned into the bar. Wine already gone, she sipped water from her straw, as she jabbed at what little ice remained in her near tepid water. She wished that she had never said the word wife, but now it was too late, and she couldn't take it back.

"One Saturday night, I came home around ten o'clock. It had been a shitty day and I was tired, and headed straight for the shower. Julie brought me a beer and said, 'I have to go out and get a lottery ticket.' I said, are you kidding? She laughed and said, 'No, I forgot to get one earlier today.' I said, do you want me to go? She said, 'No, I'll get it, I'll be right back,' and poked her head into the shower for a kiss. I was glad. I was tired, and the last thing I wanted was to go back out again."

"What happened?" Grace said, reaching the bottom of her glass, and wishing John would interrupt the awkwardness with at least an offer to refill her water, if not her Chardonnay. No such luck, his head was buried in the game.

"I let her go. I fucking let her go."

Finally, John looked her way. Thank God for commercials. "Chardonnay please," Grace said in what came out as almost a nervous whisper. "And more water."

"Sure," John said. Noticing that Rehnquist had barely touched his drink, John asked, "Nick, Cosmo okay?" Rehnquist answered with a quick thumbs up. *Huh, must be slowing down for the evening,* John thought.

"I got out of the shower and threw on some clothes, grabbed my beer, and went into the living room and turned on the TV. I sat there and flipped through the channels, trying to find something intelligent in the mindless dribble. After a while I realized that it was now almost eleven, and Julie should have been home. It was past the Lotto cut-off time, and our Circle K was just a couple of miles away.

Grace sat back and picked nervously at her bar napkin, still wishing she could be anywhere but here.

"Here ya go," John said, returning with two glasses water and Grace's wine. Sensing the tension of the moment he had topped Grace's glass just shy of the rim.

"Thank you," she said quietly.

"When she didn't come home, I called her cell phone. It rang several times, and then went to voicemail. Then I got scared. I called her again and again, but I only got her voicemail. I threw on my pants and drove to the Circle K. It was surrounded by police cars and yellow tape. I ran up to the store but was stopped by two officers before I could get there." Rehnquist paused, poured back his Cosmo, and motioned for another. John answered by holding up the shaker. *So much for slowing down.*

For a moment Rehnquist was quiet, at a loss for words, in search of the strength to continue. Once he found it, he continued. He remained calm, but his expression revealed the extent of his restrained anger. "She walked in on a robbery." Some fuckwad went in before her to rob the jackass at the register, and she was at the wrong place, at the wrong time. The asshole freaked. No one was in the convenience store, and this guy walked in and was robbing the clerk. He was holding a gun on him when Julie walked in. He spooked and shot him. I can only suppose that he killed Julie because she was witness to it all."

"Oh my God!" Grace exclaimed. "Did they catch the guy?"

"No," Rehnquist said, shifting his gaze to the lemon peel resting at the bottom of his glass. "The convenience store, like all convenience stores, dumped their cash into a floor safe, so they had no cash. Apparently, the clerk was running a gambling parlor on the side, with lots of cash, and the robber knew it. The clerk was the night manager, and understood the security system. He knew that no one watched the security cameras—that they were there in case they were robbed, of course—but the recordings were then kept for a month to deter employee theft. He didn't want his little side action recorded, so he disabled the camera at the cashier's counter. So, all we—I mean—all the police—have is a grainy video of the backside of someone running from the store in a black hoodie."

"How long has it been?"

"Almost five years. Not a day goes by, I don't miss her."

"I can't image. How have you survived?" *Jesus, did I really say that? How could I be so stupid?*

"I don't know," Rehnquist said, burying his face in his hands. I live one day at a time. For years, I spent my life looking for the ghost in the hoodie that killed my wife. It consumed me. Today? I don't know."

"And the department?"

"I was asked to leave, but it was my own fault. I couldn't get my shit together." Rehnquist dropped his hands and turned toward Grace, his face softening a bit. "It was all I could think about. I couldn't focus on work, and all I wanted to do was look for her killer." He turned back to the bar and picked up his fresh Cosmo. "Not to mention the drinking . . ."

Grace glanced down at her watch and gave the band a quick tug. It was a terrible time to leave, but she thought that Rehnquist needed his space, and could use the time alone. So she sat there in silence and finished her wine. After a few moments she reached into her purse for her credit card, which she slid across the bar to get John's attention, and to settle the tab.

"I got this," Rehnquist said.

"Not tonight Nick, tonight is on me," she said, pointing to Rehnquist and herself. John nodded.

"Thank you Grace, it was a pleasure to see you again," John said, when he handed her the check.

"No John, the pleasure is mine," she said, wishing it were true. She paid the check and then turned to Rehnquist and gave him a short, if not awkward hug. "It's getting late," she said. "I'd best be going. Promise me you won't drive."

"Don't worry, I won't. I'll catch a cab."

"Promise?"

Rehnquist nodded.

Grace bent down and gave him a kiss on the cheek. The non-threatening kind of kiss that a departing friend leaves you with. "I'm sorry," she whispered.

"Thank you," he said, not looking up. When he finally did, she was gone.

Another man in his position might have accepted Grace's invitation to spend the night at Jason's, and see where the night might have led. Rehnquist had a pretty good idea, and he wasn't willing to go there—no reason to put either of them through that. Better to have told Grace about Julie here at the bar, than to have to tell her later, at the worst possible time.

Rehnquist liked Grace as soon as he met her, that first night when she asked for his help. He wasn't sure what it was, but there was just something about her—the way she made him feel, and that's what worried him.

She was beautiful, but so were a lot of other women he knew—and he certainly didn't feel the same way about them. No, there was something more, and it hurt to admit to himself that he was attracted to her. If he were ever to love another woman . . . but then he reminded himself that he would not. He wasn't ready, and didn't expect that he ever would be—not even Grace. And beyond love, he reasoned that any lust he felt was primal; he couldn't imagine ever having a serious relationship with another woman, much less being intimate.

He meant it when he said 'forever,' and Julie would forever be his soulmate. He thought about her constantly, and didn't need the damn nightmares to remind him of his pain, or his love for her. Even today, almost five years later, there were days when the pain felt as deep, and as fresh as the night he lost her, and if anything, he loved her more with each passing day.

Once this business with Jason was over, he would do his best to keep Grace as a close friend. He really enjoyed being around her, and he could use someone to talk to. He wasn't close to many people, and over the years he had pushed most of his close friends away. He didn't want that to happen with Grace, and he'd do his best to keep her close—just not too close.

"John, one more," Rehnquist said, pointing to his glass, "Then you'd better call me a cab."

"Are you sure?" John asked, not quite sure if he should serve him.

"No, I guess you're right. Time for a change. Single malt whisky—twelve-year-old."

John sat a glass of water in front of Rehnquist and said, "Time to hydrate."

"Hydrate? I stay plenty hydrated, what with all the ice you put it your drinks."

"Really?" John scowled. "I'd think that man that drinks as much as you wouldn't want to piss off his bartender."

"Naw, I'm just shittin' you." Rehnquist took a quick sip from the tall glass and snorted, "Shit! That's what water tastes like? I'll stick to the good stuff," pointing to the top shelf.

"Good to know. A man would never wanna piss off his bartender."

Rehnquist pulled the printout out of his back pocket and unfolded it onto the bar. *Just one more look.*

John watched him for a moment and then cautiously poured two fingers of Scotch in a shallow glass, and slid it in front of Rehnquist.

"Thanks John, you're the best"

"I bet you say that to all your bartenders."

"No John, just you," he said with a wink.

John started walk away, but stopped and turned around. "Nick, I make a point of not listening to my patrons' conversations, but I've got ears, and I couldn't help but overhear. I'm sorry, you have my condolences."

"Thank you," Rehnquist said, and frowned. "Some days are better than others; today is not one of those days."

John nodded and went back to work, wiping down the display bottles in preparation to close.

Rehnquist stuck his nose in the glass and took a long whiff, as if he knew shit about Scotch. "Smoky, with hint of peat," he said, almost pleased with himself as he slowly touched the amber liquid to his lips. He didn't even like Scotch, and wasn't sure why he ordered it. *Guess I'm just bored.* As he set the glass back down, he looked up at John and said, "Ahhh, twelve-year-old Scotch. John, that reminds me of a joke—and then, I'll take that cab."

Rehnquist told his joke and then sat back starring half cross-eyed at the printout, while the whisky slowly evaporated into his soul. "Time to go buddy, let's call it a night." John said."

"Okay," Rehnquist said, fumbling a credit card across the bar while he continued to stare at the printout.

"You've got no tab. Grace got the first one, and the Scotch is on me."

"Thank you," Rehnquist said, extending his hand.

John shook it, and said, "Hope to see you again."

"You will. I'll be back in a couple days, as soon as my liver needs punished again."

"It's a date Nick—"

Rehnquist sat up straight, startled for a second, staring at the printout. "Holy shit! You're right! It *is* a date. You're a fucking genius! I could just kiss you."

"That's okay Nick, maybe next time. Besides, cab's here."

Chapter Twenty

Rehnquist awoke to the sound of his ringing phone and a pounding headache. He sat up, completely disorientated, and was clueless as to where he was. The clock radio on the far bedside table said 8:36 a.m. He looked around the room for a moment, trying to orientate himself. The room was almost completely dark, with just a little light coming in from around the window drapes. He reached next to him and felt for the bedside table lamp, and then fumbled for the switch, which he eventually found, and turned on the light. He was still in the shirt that he had worn the night before, and his pants were lying crumpled on the floor beside the bed. He stumbled to his feet and picked up his pants, and rummaged through the pockets in search of his phone. No phone. *Shit. Hope I didn't lose it. Oh wait, I just heard it.*

He looked on the loveseat and on the chair in the corner. No phone. It also wasn't on the dresser, or on the desk. He eventually found it behind the ice bucket on the sink, with about five percent charge remaining. Four missed calls from Grace, and three voicemails. Rehnquist went to the bathroom before returning Grace's call, and he decided to call her first, and then listen to the voicemails later. As he was waiting for the phone to ring he looked at himself in the mirror. *I look like shit. No wonder I feel this bad.*

Grace answered on the second ring. "Where are you?"

"In my room."

"Are you alright?"

"I'm not sure, I haven't taken a complete inventory yet."

"Last night you said you'd be up and on your way by seven, and then you'd call me."

"I did?"

"Nick, I talked to you when you were in the cab—in a text. Don't you remember?"

"Not really . . . Wait, I think it's coming back to me."

"I thought you were upset with me and that's why you weren't answering my calls."

"Upset? Why would I be upset?" Then it occurred to him, their conversation about Julie. "If you mean about Julie, why—"

"I don't know, but when you didn't answer . . ."

"Grace, I'm sorry. I was sleeping and didn't hear my phone ring until the last time, and then I couldn't find it."

"How much did you have to drink last night?"

"I don't know—too much, but it was worth it. After you left, I figured out the numbers—well not all the numbers, just part of them. Well I didn't figure it out, John did—well not exactly. It's something he said that got me to thinking. *He wished he could remember what.*

"Nick, you're rambling and not making any sense."

"Grace, my phone is almost dead. Let me charge it and grab a quick shower, I'll call you back on my way to the Keys."

"What about your appointments up here? — Going back to the school?"

"I'm bagging those—at least for today. This thing with the numbers is way more important, and I've got to figure out the rest of it."

Rehnquist put his phone on the charger, grabbed a shower and made a cup of hotel in-room coffee. While his phone was charging, he looked back to yesterday's text with Grace. *Shit, I don't remember any of this. Glad I didn't say anything inappropriate.* During his shower he had replayed the evening several times, trying to piece together his conversation with John. When he cleaned out the pockets of his pants and found the folded up printout, he remembered. Now mostly firing on all cylinders, he looked at the numbers carefully. *'052314'— could be a date. But what's its significance, and what about the rest of the series of numbers?*

Rehnquist checked out and grabbed a second cup of coffee in the hotel lobby, but waited until he was headed down the Stretch to call Grace. Most importantly, he waited until he could pull himself together, remember last night's Eureka moment, and compose a semi-intelligent sentence.

"Grace, I'm sorry about oversleeping and not answering your calls."

"You had me worried."

"Please, don't worry about the conversation about Julie. Besides, you didn't ask, I told you."

"I should never have said what I said to put you in that awkward situation. You kind of had to say something."

"First, I'm flattered—wait. I'm sorry, that didn't come out right. Maybe I misread the chemistry at the bar last night—"

"You didn't."

"Well, then I am flattered." Rehnquist smiled. *Still got it.*

"I don't know what happened," Grace said. She flushed with embarrassment, and was glad he wasn't there to see her. "Maybe it was just the excitement of the good news about Jason. I felt better—happy and more relaxed—than I have in a long time."

"Oh, I thought it was me."

"It was you, you big turd. I'm sorry, I'll be on my best behavior from now on."

"I certainly hope not, that would be boring . . . Grace, about Julie, maybe it was good for me to talk about it—about her. Outside of George and occasionally Betty, I rarely do. I keep it bottled up, and it's very rare for me to open up to anyone else. When I do, it has to be someone I really trust for me to let down my defenses and let go of my emotions—even when I'm drinking."

"You *can* trust me, Nick. Beyond whatever's happened to Jason, I consider us friends now. Anytime you want, or need to talk, please call, I'm a good listener."

"Yes you are, you proved that last night. Thank you."

Chapter Twenty-One

Hope was very excited to see Rehnquist when he arrived home. "Missed me, huh?" He fed her and gave her fresh water, and stayed with her while she ate, lightly stroking her back as she purred. Then he went inside, brewed a cup of coffee, and booted his laptop at the kitchen table, in preparation for what he assumed would be a long day. He sat down and logged onto his computer and opened the folder with Jason's files, sorting them by date and searched for 5/23/2014. Nothing. Then he put 052314 into Windows Search. It returned two emails and thirty file names beginning with 052314: the black and white photos that Jason had sent Grace.

He opened the folder that contained these photos, and checked the properties on several. There was nothing unique there, just the standard properties that would be found on any scanned photo. Then he opened the first one in the series, 052314_00000. This was a photo of a bride and groom standing in front of a car model that he didn't recognize, that appeared to be from the late '40s or early '50s. *Must be Grace's grandparents.*

He opened the image in Photoshop, and zoomed in to 200%, scrolling back and forth, and up and down looking for anything unique, just as he had on the earlier duplicate dockside photographs that Jason had emailed to Grace. Next he tried enhancing the image by lightening shadows and decreasing midtone contrast, which brought out details which were not previously visible. He zoomed in to 400%, and carefully began scrolling once again. After a moment, he saw it. Down near the bottom right corner of the photo, in an area dense with grass, were three characters superimposed over the image, w0+. He reset the enhancement settings, and the characters were completely hidden within the grass.

The next image in the series was 052314_00002, another picture of the bride and groom in front of the same car, but from a different angle. He opened it, enhanced it as he had on the first one, zoomed in, and found another three-character set, y>', this one hidden in the shadow of the car.

Rehnquist pondered the possibilities over his next cup of coffee. He could only surmise that the numbers separated by hyphens which followed the date on Jason's duplicate photo, corresponded to the image names of the black and white photos, and the order in which to place the hidden character sets. *But then what? The long string of characters must be password—hopefully to Jason's Syncquest account.*

He systematically opened each of the photos referenced in the series of numbers. All contained a hidden, three-digit character set in roughly the same location, except four. He worked with those four extensively and tried everything he could think of, and no matter how he modified the images, he couldn't find any hidden character sets.

Rehnquist made a spreadsheet with the photo numbers in one column and the character sets in the column next to them. As expected, he was four character sets short. He started to go back and take another look at the four images that didn't appear to have any hidden codes, and then he remembered the four black and white photos that were attached to Jason's original email, the one where he had just begun to scan and cleanup the photos. These were copies of four on the shared drive— well maybe. He had learned about Jason's copies. He opened the folder containing the four photographs. He smiled when he realized that the numbers of the photographs corresponded to the four that he was missing. *Coincidence? Unlikely.*

Rehnquist opened the first of the photos, enlarged it, and did his Photoshop magic. Bingo. There it was; likewise, on the other three. Jason obviously made certain that the link to the shared drive alone was not enough. You also had to have the four photos from the

first email. He combined the character sets together into two strings, and then combined them into one long string:
H4*5+c">iw0+UR8)oCiDl::7K6#iDly>'H4*)%6T@Uu %9[zfw0+U'f]!C5+c

He went to the Syncquest website, clicked Account Login, and typed in Jason's email address. Then he copied and pasted the character string into the password field, and clicked 'Login.' The browser window paused for a second and then opened to two parent folders. "Sonofabitch," Rehnquist said aloud. An hour later he was on his way to purchase an external hard drive, and on the phone to Grace. "The number *was* a date," he said. Then he explained about the hidden character sets, how he came to find them, and how he was able to login to Jason's files.

Grace was surprised and elated. "What did you use for a user name?"

"His email address."

"But his account's inactive."

"He would only have to have a valid email address to set up the account, after which it becomes his username."

"Oh."

"There's a lot of data on the drive, in two parent folders. The first is a backup of Jason's computer, the second appears to be just storage. It's named "'MDCPS,' and is full of school district related files. Collectively they both occupy about half a terabyte of space. I'm driving up to Key Largo to buy an external hard drive now, so I can download copies of the files; otherwise, it would take forever to go through them all, live on the internet.

"Why would Jason go to so much trouble to hide a password? It's either sheer generous or pure luck that you figured it out. He couldn't have left those for clues." Grace said.

"I don't think he did—just the opposite. I think they're breadcrumbs for him."

"What do you mean?"

"He needed some way that he could inactivate his email account and completely detach himself from all his electronics—even if it meant destroying them or wiping them clean—and still have a route back into his cloud storage. All he needed was your copies of those four emails, and he knew you'd still have them. He knew you wouldn't delete emails with photos attached."

"Normally I wouldn't, but he's lucky that I didn't delete the second email with the picture at George's house."

"Guess that was a bit of a gamble on his part. That said, I would have thought that he would have used a more secure method of hiding his password—or at least encrypted it. Maybe he *did* want to leave behind clues, just in case . . ."

"Go ahead, you can say it."

"I'm sorry Grace."

"Me too," Grace said. Rehnquist could hear the despair in her voice. "You said completely detach himself. You don't think he's accessed his account recently?"

"No. As far as I can tell—based upon the file modification dates—the last time his computer or any device was in contact with the backup files or the school district files was the day before he disappeared—which is about the same time that he shut down his email account, and turned off his phone, effectively becoming incommunicado. Unless he intentionally disabled the backup on his computer, it would have made a connection with the server every time that his computer was on and had a Wi-Fi connection."

"Surely he had Wi-Fi at the hotel."

"It would have been available, but that doesn't mean he used it. That or he did, and he disabled the backups, or he hasn't turned on his computer—if he even has it. One thing I am sure of, since he could log on from anywhere—like I just did—he doesn't want to have contact with the server."

"Why? What possible explanation is there?"

"I don't know, maybe the answers are somewhere in his files. Okay, I'm here now. I'll call you later, hopefully with some news."

Chapter Twenty-Two

Forty minutes later Rehnquist was home, had the external hard drive hooked up, and was downloading documents from Jason's backup folder. Two-hour estimation on the backup downloads, then the district files. He looked at his phone. *Plenty of time to kill, think I'll hit the gym.* It had been over a week and he had zero motivation, but other than that, he had no reason not to go. He ate a protein bar, changed into workout clothes, grabbed a backpack with toiletries and a change of clothes and drove the few miles north to the gym.

The twenty-minute warmup on the treadmill didn't do anything to help his motivation level, but he endeavored to push through thirty minutes of upper body, followed by fifteen minutes of squats. Then he showered and changed clothes, and on his way home stopped by the deli and picked up a corned beef on rye. Then he took advantage of the last few miles drive home to call and check on George and Betty. George was inbound from a half day of fishing with two long time clients from Upstate New York. He said the clients were happy—so he was happy—and they were all headed to the Lorelei.

"Care to join us?"

"I'd love to George, but I have work to do. Some other time."

"Okay. If you change your mind, you know where to find us."

"You bet."

Meanwhile, Jason's documents had finished downloading, so Rehnquist started downloading the school district folder, in its entirety. There had to be something in there. Another gut feeling, to be sure, but his previous gut feelings had served him well. Only problem is that the estimated download time was over ten hours.

Rehnquist grabbed a beer and unwrapped his sandwich, and began poking around in Jason's downloaded documents while he ate. Jason's folders and documents looked just like his condo and his safe deposit box. He was clearly a neatness freak, which in this case was great. Every individual file was logically titled and organized. Financial statements were all downloaded pdfs, organized by account name, then into individual folders by year.

The level of organization made for fast, easy work, and within a couple hours Rehnquist concluded that Jason rarely used his credit cards, and when he did, he paid every bill in full at the end of the month. For the most part, his records went back five or six years, depending upon the account, and Rehnquist could only find a single time when he paid finance charges.

Rehnquist couldn't find copies of checking or savings account statements; however, the backup folder contained a copy of a Quicken file. Chances are Jason maintained those accounts electronically—as did Rehnquist—and just never bothered to download monthly pdf statements.

He wrapped up his assessment of Jason's finances by looking at Jason's brokerage statements. These were for an IRA that he was maintaining in addition to the school's pension system, and up until the time when he left the school, he was putting two hundred dollars a paycheck into it. By all appearances, Jason was frugal and managed his finances well, but mostly Rehnquist was relieved to see that there was no obvious evidence of financial shenanigans.

Rehnquist wanted to begin looking at the school district files; unfortunately, the time he had spent looking at the files that he had already downloaded bogged down the hard drive and the second download, and it still had over nine hours remaining. Time for a long break, another beer, his book, and an unexpected, but well-deserved nap.

An hour or so later Rehnquist awoke, startled, in his recliner to a knock on the door, followed by the sound of the door opening, and George saying, "Honey, I'm home."

Rehnquist sat up and rubbed his eyes. "What time is it?"

"A little after five. How long you been asleep?" Rehnquist shrugged and sat up in his chair. George held up a large to go container, set it on the counter, and said, "Brought you some fish, yellowtail and grouper. The yellowtail is grilled, and the grouper is lightly blackened. Not my choice, but it's pretty good."

"Today's catch?"

"Yes. My customers are flying out early tomorrow morning, so they sent this home with me, and I thought that you could use a good meal. Maybe you'd like to try something healthy for a change."

"I eat healthy. What's with everybody?"

"Healthy? Burgers, wings—"

"Okay, okay."

"and," George said, opening the refrigerator door to help himself to a beer, "just show me one thing healthy in here. Hell, you don't even have any decent beer," as he pulled out two Stellas.

"Healthy's in your hand—but thanks for dinner."

George sat one beer on the counter, tore the paper wrap from around the top of the other, and fumbled trying to twist off the cap.

"George, that's real beer—no twist offs. The opener's on the freezer door," Rehnquist said, thoroughly amused.

George just shrugged. Rehnquist stood up and walked into the kitchen, just as George popped the top on the second beer and handed to him.

"Don't know why they have to be so damned inconvenient."

Rehnquist shook his head. "George, you're incorrigible."

George sat down on the side of the kitchen table in front of the computer, and Rehnquist took a seat at the end beside him. George tilted his head, smiled, and gave Rehnquist a shit-eating grin. "So, sleeping old man?

Rehnquist looked over lethargically. "I worked out today—and I kicked my own ass. And, I didn't sleep well very well last night."

"Why?"

Rehnquist told George about the exchange with Grace, and his overindulgence.

"How'd she take that?"

"Not well. She was pretty uncomfortable—from what I remember. But as I told her this morning, the fact that I opened up to her says a lot about her. Obviously I trust her."

"She's a good woman, you *can* trust her." George looked at the computer on the table, hard drive connected to a USB port, spinning away. "What's with this?"

Rehnquist peeked around to see the screen, moused-over the file transfer dialog box, and looked at the download time remaining. Then he gave George a quick rundown of how he managed to get into Jason's files, and how relieved he was to see that his finances at least looked spotless. "We'll see what I find in the other folder. Only seven more hours to go on the download. Guess that'll be tomorrow morning's project."

George finished his beer and said, "Well, I'd better be going and get cleaned up, Betty wants Italian tonight." He smiled broadly and shook Rehnquist's hand, "Although after the late lunch, I may have to settle for an appetizer."

"Thanks again for the fish, and give my love to Betty. I'll let you know what I find out."

Chapter Twenty-Three

Rehnquist decided to forgo his usual morning run and start right away on the school district folder. He made himself a cup of coffee and sat down at the kitchen table in front of the computer. Last night, before going to bed, he texted Grace to give her an update on the progress of the download, and said it will be at least tomorrow morning before I can get a look at those files. After verifying that the download was complete, he checked to see if there were any changes to the modification dates on the folders—there wasn't—then he logged off the website, closed the browser, and clicked open the folder named 'MDCPS.' Next he texted Grace and said 'The download is complete, I'll let you know what I find out.'

Not surprisingly, Jason's level of organization and file naming extended to this folder as well, and it contained several subfolders, many of which contained additional subfolders. The first subfolder was named 'Logs,' and within it were two subfolders. The first, 'Network,' was filled with many months of daily network connection logs from hundreds of different computers. These were long text files with thousands of rows of network connections and disconnections, each with the computer's name, IP and MAC addresses, and the user's name.

The second subfolder was named 'Sanchez,' and contained dozens of daily usage logs for a specific user, 'rsanchez,' from two different MAC addresses, so he surmised the logs were from two different computers. One of these, which he assumed must be a desktop, always used the same IP address. The second had several different IP addresses, and must be a laptop, accessing the network or internet from remote locations. Apparently these files were important to Jason, but not so much to Rehnquist. Maybe if he analyzed the history long enough, he could find a trend or something interesting, but at first glance most of the history was internal, from the school's intranet, and the external web addresses didn't look too crazy—no obvious porn or anything like that.

Rehnquist backed out of the folder and its parent, and went to the second folder in 'MDCPS.' It contained many subfolders, each filled with voluminous pdf files of building construction requests for proposals, respondent submissions, bid tabulation scoresheets, change requests, and agenda summaries for bid disqualifications. He chose a construction RFP at random, opened it, and scrolled through it. It was for a new elementary school and the specifications were mind-boggling; well beyond his knowledge of building construction. He closed it, and opened the accompanying bid scoresheet. Fourteen companies bid on the project.

The company that scored the highest, and the one that the staff recommend, was Grupo Domingo, even though there were two lower bids. The Grupo Domingo bid was for $8.4 million, almost $300 thousand more than the lowest bid, and about $175 thousand more than the second lowest. Two project managers and a procurement analyst scored the bids. The lead project manager was Rodolfo Sanchez, and as Rehnquist was about to find out when he opened the next file, Sanchez also wrote the board agenda summaries for the disqualifications.

Rehnquist spent the next few hours opening RFPs, respondent submissions, and bid scoresheets. Grupo Domingo was awarded the bid on most of them, even though they frequently were not the lowest bidder. Several times when they were not awarded the bid, it went to Palmway Construction, when Palmway was the lowest bidder. Other than Grupo Domingo and occasionally Palmway Construction, Rodolfo Sanchez was the common denominator in all of them.

Rehnquist took a short break, stretched, gave up the coffee for a beer, and went right back to work. The next folder was titled 'Notes.' In it was a series of Word documents, which Rehnquist spent the next two hours reading, and then re-reading. They told him everything he needed to know—and then some. The other folders in 'MDCPS,' including the one filled with hundreds of pages of pdf printouts of the rsanchez emails could wait. Time to call Grace.

Chapter Twenty-Four

"Hello Nick."

"Grace, where are you?"

"I'm at Jason's, getting ready to go see my mother."

"Can you talk?"

"Yes, why?"

"Because I need your full, undivided attention—otherwise this won't make any sense—and I definitely wouldn't want to have this conversation with you if you were driving. I'd prefer to talk in person, but I can't afford the driving time today, and this can't wait—I want you to know what's going on."

"What is it Nick?"

"First, let me apologize if this is a little sketchy. I've spent the morning buried in the school board folder in Jason's computer files, and I'm just beginning to understand it myself—and that's only because Jason kept a detailed journal that explains what he did, and what he found out. His journal also references documents, emails, and files to support his case—all of which are also contained within his files. I'll give you the Reader's Digest version.

"Okay—I think."

"So, back in his days with the school board, Jason stumbled into a mess, and the more he looked into it, the deeper he got. Basically, without benefit of law enforcement, he was conducting his own cyber investigation."

Grace had been standing in the bathroom brushing her hair when Rehnquist called. When he said 'cyber investigation' she put down the brush, walked into the living room, and sat down on the loveseat.

"When Jason was the network administrator, in addition to maintaining the infrastructure of the network, his major responsibilities were to prevent network intrusion, data theft or corruption, and the introduction of viruses into their system. Quite a job if you think about it—all the places students might happen across on any given day. Anyway, Jason routinely monitored network traffic looking for potential aberrancies, and one day he came across a report that showed a computer had remotely accessed the network via an IP address from Columbia.

"I don't totally understand the mechanics of all of this, but in order for the computer to be able to connect to the district's network remotely, the network had to be able to identify and authenticate both the computer and the user—regardless of their physical location. The system by which it does this also allowed Jason to ID the user, who was Rodolfo Sanchez. Sanchez is a senior construction project manager at the district. Jason checked, and Sanchez was on vacation—presumably in Columbia."

While Rehnquist talked, he opened another beer, then opened the blinds in his living room. It was a typical Keys day outside, beautiful; unfortunately, what he had just learned left a big, black cloud hanging over it.

"Over the course of the next four days, Sanchez's computer connected four more times, once each day. Jason was immediately suspicious, and wondered why Sanchez would be connecting with the school system's network every day while he was on vacation. So, by the second day, he began to monitor Sanchez's traffic, and what internal and internet addresses he was accessing while he was connected. Basically, Sanchez was reviewing the status of project bids. More specifically, those bids which involved large projects." Rehnquist paused for sip

202

of beer, while Grace impatiently waited for the ball to drop.

"Jason continued to monitor Sanchez's computer use after he returned from vacation and he began to spot some patterns. Sanchez was instrumental in awarding bids for large construction projects to Grupo Domingo, a large Miami based construction company. It appeared that he ensured that a disproportionate number of large bids went to Grupo Domingo, often by disqualifying lower bidders.

"Sometimes Grupo Domino *was* the low bidder; however, when they were, they had a history of cost overruns and using change orders which increased the actual price of projects by five to ten percent or more. When Grupo Domingo didn't win the bid, it often went to a smaller company, Palmway Construction. Together, Grupo Domingo and Palmway Construction build, and have built, many of the district's new schools, and they also handle a fair percentage of their large-scale school renovations. . . . You with me?"

"Yes. So far it sounds like a typical, everyday Miami public official and vendor collusion."

"That's what I thought—at first. Okay, so here's where it gets ugly. Since Jason was an IT administrator, he had access to all of the school system's computers, in addition to the network. He configured keystroke logging software to automatically download and install on

Sanchez's computer, which he then used to monitor his activity on the school's computer, both when he was on the school's network, and also when he was home or on some other network."

"My God Nick, that's illegal! He—"

"Hold on," he interrupted. Actually the courts have been divided on this. It all depends on when Sanchez was using the computer, and if the school had some expectation of him working at the time, regardless of whether it was on property, from home, or on a business trip. The argument would be that they own the computer and he was working at the time. They must surely also have a policy with regard to personal use of computers and the school district's rights to monitor that use, which somewhere down the line Sanchez probably acknowledged in writing."

"Now you sound like an attorney, and somehow that doesn't make me feel any better."

"I understand. Well, anyway, here's the deal breaker. Obviously monitoring internal network traffic *was* legal and probably justified in order to protect the school system's network, the problem is that Jason's surveillance eventually included the interception of Sanchez's email on his personal account. That certainly crossed the line, even though Jason had reason to believe that Sanchez was involved in something illegal."

Suddenly Grace felt quite ill. She could feel a lump rise in her throat, and her eyes begin to tear up.

"That said, Jason learned that Grupo Domingo contracts with several subcontractors to provide various construction services. These subcontractors provide skilled and non-skilled laborers ranging from electricians, plumbers, roofers, drywallers, painters, and landscapers. For the most part, these contractors all have a couple of things in common. They are small, and they are minority owned—at least on paper. They help Domingo to conform with the school system's small contractor preference and minority ownership bidding requirements. Most importantly—at least for Domingo—they provide an easy avenue for money laundering and tax evasion." Rehnquist paused for another sip.

"But what does this have to do with Jason?" Grace asked, her patience fading.

"Hear me out, I'll get there. Grupo Domingo is paid by the school system, via check or electronic funds transfer, and then they pay the subcontractors. Nothing unusual there. What is unusual, is that the subs deposit the funds, and then they pay the majority of their laborers cash, tax-free and unreported. The laborers are, as you might have guessed, illegal immigrants, who are all too happy to receive unreported cash."

Grace got up and poured herself a generous glass of Scotch and began to pace the floor. *Jason is such a little shit. Wait 'til I see him.*

Rehnquist continued, "For the most part, the subcontractors are shell corporations, with a few paid officers, administrative personnel and a handful of legitimate laborers for show. The vast majority of the actual workers are working for cash, off the books. It appears that most of the reported and unreported profits from these corporations are transferred to offshore banks, or are being invested in Central and South American real estate and construction projects, through a tangled web of Panamanian and Cayman banks.

"What Jason figured out is that the cash used to pay the workers originates from two sources, either drug sales in the US from drugs smuggled in across the border, or from human smuggling—often the workers themselves. Effectively the subcontractors are being used to launder drug and smuggling money, move it out of the county into legitimate investments, and evade US taxes."

"And just how did he reach that conclusion?"

"That's where the emails come in. Apparently Sanchez isn't the sharpest tack in the box when it comes to technology. Incriminating emails from an obscure Yahoo account to other obscure Yahoo accounts, but on a school computer. What a dumbass. One thing for certain, Sanchez is no mastermind. It looks like he's a lapdog, and does what he's told. Jason was looking for a connection to someone simply referred to as 'Red,' who was mentioned from time to time in the dozens of emails that Jason intercepted and recorded. He believed that Red ran and controlled the entire operation, was the hands on guy, and the enforcer."

"This is terrible Nick. Do you think Sanchez figured out he was being monitored?"

"I don't think so—at least not at first. It looks like where Jason got into trouble was that he didn't just sit behind the keyboard. Once he left the school district he started talking with many of the workers. He'd meet up with them at bus stops, or neighborhood cafes, and over time he earned their trust."

"Jesus, what was he thinking? He must have lost his mind."

"The workers are from Venezuela, Columbia, Central America, and Mexico. They were smuggled in— presumably by Domingo affiliates—after it was determined that they had the skills necessary to work once they got here. Kind of a human resources recruiting/smuggling operation. And by work, I mean for Grupo Domingo—at least the skilled ones. Once they were here, papers were provided for many of them, but only after they earned them. Also, they all came without their families, with the promise that once they were established and proved their worth as an employee, their families would be brought here too."

Rehnquist finished his beer, and while he continued talking, he opened another.

"It looks like the family part rarely happened—just often enough to give the other workers hope that someday it would happen for them. The reality is that many of the lower skilled workers are indentured servants—having agreed to work off the cost of their migration. Many of these end up working in landscaping and agriculture, and regardless of where they work, a big portion of their pay goes back to paying for either their trip across the border, or toward their families' future migration. Many of the higher skilled workers paid their costs upfront—cash of course—which was exchanged for dollars and paid right back to them and the other workers. Something ironic about that."

Grace took a sip of her Scotch, and felt a shiver run down her spine. She just couldn't believe that Jason could be so brash and foolish.

"Is this as bad as it sounds?" she asked.

"Unfortunately, yes. Thank God his notes are meticulous, and it looks like he has the documentation to back it up."

"And all of this is going on in broad daylight, and nobody catches on? . . . only Jason?"

"Remember Grace, we're talking Miami. People see what they want to see, or don't see what they don't want to see. Some people are paid not to see. The president and majority shareholder of Grupo Domingo is Juan Pablo Rojas. Rojas is a naturalized Columbian who came here with his parents when he was a small child. According to his bio on Domingo's website, Rojas's father began his life in the US as a humble construction worker, and eventually ended up owning his own general contracting company.

"The old man insisted that his children receive a proper education and sent them to a number of private schools. Rojas worked for his father throughout school and after he graduated. Then, after his father died, he went to work for other contractors in various capacities, mostly on medium to good sized projects: Fire stations, small office buildings, and strip malls. Along the way, he made his mark on the construction industry, and got to know a number of influential people. He has a great bio, write-ups in local business magazines, good reviews, and even a short video on YouTube. On the surface, Rojas is quite the gentleman, perfect in manner and speech—but he has a dark side.

"About ten years ago, Rojas started Grupo Domingo with the help of hired talent where he didn't have the expertise. These were engineers, project managers and the like. Today, on paper at least, Grupo Domingo is a multimillion dollar corporation, but who knows how big they really are. And, in addition to the Miami-Dade school system, they also have contracts with the county, Palm Beach and Broward Counties, and with several local municipalities."

"What about the other company?" Grace asked. "Palm . . . what was it?

"Palmway Construction. They and all the subcontractors are Subchapter S corporations, so, other than the names of a few majority shareholders who meet the minority requirements for bidding, the names of most of the shareholders are not public. Undoubtedly Rojas is one, or at least he has some financial interest in them, on paper or off. Jason was also looking at that.

"Jason figured out that in order for this operation to work, it must involve a lot of people. At the school system alone, cost overruns and change orders had to be approved at the highest levels—most at the level of the school board. And justification is required to disqualify a lower bid. Sanchez wrote the disqualifications, but they had to be signed off by at least one other project manager, a procurement officer, and the department head.

"According to Jason's journal, he was getting ready to turn his files over to the Feds. He was actually scheduled to meet with Reuben Anders, an ICE special agent, at the Starbucks at the corner of Palm and US 1 the day after he disappeared."

"Starbucks?"

"Safe, neutral ground, I guess. Jason had to be careful. He needed to filter his information as not to incriminate himself."

"Why ICE?"

"I don't know, I'm not sure where I would go with it. This one is complicated: drug smuggling, human trafficking, money laundering, and tax evasion—just for starters. There are probably a dozen different federal agencies with jurisdiction here."

"His appointment? I wonder if he made it."

"I don't think so. He intercepted an email from Sanchez the morning of the day he disappeared. They were on to him. That's why I don't think that Sanchez knew that Jason had access to his personal email account and was reading his emails. If he did, he certainly wouldn't have given him a heads up in an email that they were coming after him."

"So that's why he fled. He's lucky he wasn't killed. The ICE agent?"

"Maybe, more likely one of the workers he talked to. He was already worried, that's why he looked into selling his car the Friday before. He didn't want to risk leaving a trail . . ."

"Nick, what exactly did that email say?"

"I don't know, there isn't a copy of it with the others, and all Jason's journal entry says is 'email from Red to Rojas, JR pick up tonight.'"

Grace stopped pacing, refilled her Scotch, and sat back down on the loveseat. "Why do you think he didn't call, at least to say he was leaving for a while?"

"To protect you and your mother. Probably figured the less you knew the better, at least until he could sort it out and figure out what to do."

"But, just a quick call—"

"I don't know. Maybe he thought his phone was tapped."

"Pay phones? — there are still a few around. Or borrow a phone."

"Dunno Grace. We'll ask him when we see him."

"Okay, so now what?"

"Today, I'm going to start reading Sanchez's emails. Then tomorrow I'm driving up to see him—unannounced of course."

"Nick, please . . . be careful."

"I will. I promise. But there are a couple of other things that you need to know."

"Like what? — There's more?"

"Jason also spent some time in the newspaper archives and court records. What Rojas's dossier fails to mention is that in between the years when his father died and he started his own construction company, he was arrested three times: Twice for cocaine distribution, and once for human trafficking. None of them went to trial, even though it looks like the cops had a solid case on each of them. All three were settled nolle prosequi."

"What's that?"

"The charges were dropped. Essentially the state attorney decided not to prosecute, which is how he stayed out of jail, and how he was able to get his contractor's license."

"Have an answer for that?"

"Yes, but not a good one. Oh, and Grace, how's your Spanish?"

"Not good, why?

"I'm guessing that Jason's Spanish isn't much better. 'Rojas' is a plural derivation of rojo."

"So?"

"Rojo, 'Red.'"

Chapter Twenty-Five

For an agency that's supposed to operate in the sunshine, it's amazing that it took six phone calls just to find out the location of Sanchez's office. But persistence paid off, and Rehnquist was patiently waiting for him when he arrived back at his office after his morning construction inspections.

Sanchez walked into the reception area and dropped off some paperwork with the receptionist. They spoke for a few moments, then she told him that Mr. Rehnquist was there to see him. If Rehnquist had any question as to Sanchez being a power broker, that question was quickly answered by his handshake: limp, cold, and wet.

"Mr. Rehnquist, I'm Rodolfo Sanchez, what can I do for you?"

Nothing like a little surprise to round out your day. This should prove interesting. "Is there somewhere private we can talk?"

"We're fine here. What can I do for you?" *Dismissive. Must think I'm a salesman.*

"I'd like to speak with you about your relationship with Grupo Domingo." Suddenly Sanchez didn't look so chipper. *Ah, got his attention. A telltale twitch of the left eyelid. A nervous ringing of the hands.*

"What do you mean?"

"Are you sure you want to have this conversation here? Wouldn't you prefer a little privacy?"

"Mr. Rehnquist, if you would prefer privacy, please come back to my office."

A minute later, Rehnquist had Sanchez right where he wanted. "Mr. Sanchez, you seem to have a unique relationship with two of your vendors, Grupo Domingo and Palmway Construction. In fact, any reasonable man might think that your relationship is . . . perhaps a bit too cozy.

"What are you saying? Are you accusing me of improprieties in awarding contracts?"

"I didn't say that. It's just that most of the bids that you review go to Domingo, more often than not, as a result of multiple lower bid disqualifications. Surely you have an explanation."

"Mr. Rehnquist, I've never been so insulted. What business of yours is this, and who are you working for?"

"It's not my intention to insult you, Mr. Sanchez, and who I'm working for is immaterial; you are after all a public servant. I'm just asking for an explanation."

"I think we're done here," Sanchez said, motioning toward the door.

"No, actually I think we've just begun," Rehnquist said. "I'll be back, and I suspect that your next visit will be from someone more official. Better get ready."

Rehnquist was pleased with himself. He'd lit up a shitstorm—he'd bet on it. He got back in his car, started it, and reached under the seat for his Glock. He hadn't carried it in years, but once he read Jason's notes, he knew he would be up against some tough, desperate characters that would do anything to save their asses. He pushed the Glock into his waistband at his right flank, clipped the holster between the waistband and his belt, then pulled his shirt down over it. He had taken it out when he arrived at the school in anticipation of metal detectors. He also didn't expect anything violent out of Sanchez; Rojas was another story.

His next stop was at the main office of Grupo Domingo. Not that he expected to find Rojas there—he didn't—he just wanted to leave a business card and a request to have Rojas call him. He really didn't need to talk to him, he knew that Rojas would get the intended message, especially after Sanchez told him about their earlier encounter.

On his way back to the Keys, Rehnquist called Grace and briefed her on his morning. She knew that he was going to see Sanchez, but she didn't expect him to stop by Grupo Domingo. "Nick, you're going to get hurt. Isn't it time to involve the police?"

"Close. In fact, I brought my computer and Jason's files with me today with the expectation of meeting up with Ansco and giving him the highlights. Just enough to give him an understanding of the extent of this mess and to get his opinion on where I should go with it. Things have changed a lot these past few years with the expanding responsibilities of Homeland Security, and all of the players have changed. Everyone that I used to work with throughout the many agencies have moved on, retired, or changed positions."

"Well, are you going to meet with him?"

"Not yet. I began to have second thoughts. I think I want to copy these files over to another drive, and remove anything that potentially incriminates Jason."

"Isn't that withholding evidence?

"Yeah, something like that. Besides, I want to finish reading Sanchez's emails and see if there's anyone else that needs to be under the microscope. There're a shit load of them, and I'm less than halfway through."

After he hung up with Grace, and the more he thought about it, Rehnquist decided that he'd better at least call Ansco and give him the bullet points, leaving out the specifics of where the information came from. Just a brief rundown of the relationship between Sanchez, Grupo Domingo and Rojas, along with mentioning drug trafficking, smuggling, money laundering, and tax evasion. That way, if everything suddenly turned to shit overnight, someone else would at least be partially in the loop. Rehnquist called him and got his voicemail, so he left a message to return his call, and also asked him to check with Uber again about Jason.

Chapter Twenty-Six

Rehnquist stopped at the Tavernier Winn-Dixie on his way home to pick up a few necessities. Nothing special, just something to put in his empty refrigerator so he could have a quick meal at home without having to go out. He parked his car at the far end of the parking lot in an end space by the bank, with the hope that he wouldn't get backed into, dinged by a car door, or slammed into by a wayward shopping cart. As was his habit, he made a quick check of the car seats, dash, and floorboards for anything that might even resemble something of value.

Most of the crime in the Keys, Upper Keys at least, is crime of opportunity, rarely perpetuated by locals. It is almost always the result of day trippers from the mainland who travel down in twos or threes and make their way through parking lots looking for purses, backpacks, luggage, electronics, and shopping bags.

It's common for tourists to leave things of value out in the open, tempting even a would be thief, and worse still, they often leave their car doors unlocked, or their windows partway down so that the car won't be too hot when they return. Rehnquist could never decide if these people were just that ignorant, or if it was a combination of the southern latitude and the hot, humid salt air and blue skies that rendered them that inattentive. Upon occasion, the roving bands of thieves were even known to break out side windows to grab loose change visible in the dash or console, so it pays to be vigilant.

The only two things of value in Rehnquist's car were his computer and the external hard drive, both locked away in his trunk where he had put them that morning. He locked the car and walked toward the grocery store—but only after a brief detour to the liquor store to pick up a large bottle of Grey Goose. He was after all, shopping for necessities.

It was a quiet day for grocery shopping, with only a handful of people in the store. It wasn't usually like this, but Rehnquist was glad that it was today, and he quickly sailed through the aisles, loading his cart with a combination of healthy food and junk, and an hour later he had completed his shopping and was turning onto his street.

As he approached his house he had to drive over to the opposite side of the street in order to go around a black car that was parked on the wrong side of the road.

The car was facing him, in his lane, at the corner of his lot and his next door neighbor's. It was one of those square cars that looked more like a shoe box than it did an automobile. Rehnquist hated those cars. They might be great for hauling stuff, but they had no character. And to top it off, the driver of this car was in the car, and he was oblivious that he was on the wrong side of the street, and that he wasn't the only car on the road.

As Rehnquist approached the car he could see why the driver was oblivious. He was looking down, ball cap pulled down low over his sunglass covered eyes, and he was babbling into a cell phone. He thought about giving him a good blast of the horn to get his attention and remind him of the presence of other vehicles on the street, but thought better of it. Why bother. He'd only think that Rehnquist was an ass, and he still wouldn't understand what he was doing wrong. He carefully drove around the car and turned into his drive. As he did, he glanced at the license plate: 'Sunshine State.' *That explains it. Miami-Dade County.*

Rehnquist pulled into his drive and under his house. Once again he'd forgotten to put his reusable cloth grocery bags in the car, so he had to purchase four more at Winn-Dixie. He just couldn't handle the thought of throwing away plastic bags. He wasn't a bunny hugger, but he believed that he should leave the planet in at least as good a shape as he found it. As it was, he had four very full bags to get upstairs, two on the front passenger seat and two on the floorboard. The Grey Goose was wedged between the passenger seat and the console, and the computer and hard drive were in trunk. Two trips if he planned it right.

He slid the handles of the heaviest bag up over his left shoulder, picked up the next heaviest bag and slid it up over his right shoulder, then picked up a third bag in his left hand. That left his right hand for the house keys, so he wouldn't have to sit any of the bags down in the usual accumulation of cat hair at the top of the stairs.

As he began to ascend the stairs he saw Hope, only something was wrong. She was three quarters of the way up the stairs, and all four feet were drawn close together on the step, her back arched high, hair standing on end, trembling. Her mouth was open, teeth showing. "What's the matter girl?" Not a peep, certainly not her usual purr, and she didn't show any sign of relaxing as he came closer. *Something has scared her. Maybe a raccoon, or other large animal.*

Rehnquist looked up to the landing expecting to see a raccoon or opossum, but instead saw that his front door was slightly ajar. *Someone's in my house. That explains the car out front—and here I am with my arms full of groceries, and I can't reach my gun. They had to have heard me pull in—and they probably were alerted by the driver out front on his phone.*

Six steps to go to the top of the landing, and whatever lay inside. Rehnquist had two choices. The first was to back down the stairs, lose the groceries, get the Glock ready for the inevitable confrontation, call the cops, and then wait. But even though the sheriff's substation was just a few blocks away, chances are there were no deputies there, and by the time they arrived, who the hell knows what might happen.

Choice number two was to quickly set down the groceries right where he was, grab the Glock, storm the house and hope for the best. Since it was never like him to take the passive approach, he chose option two. He quickly pushed his keys into his pocket and set the bag in his left hand down on the step above Hope, then quietly shooed her off her step and on toward the bottom. Then, just as he reached up with his left hand to slip the bag off his right shoulder, the door burst open.

In a blur a small figure in black flew out the door and down the stairs toward him. He didn't have time to make out a face or any features, or even have time to swing a bag of groceries up as a deterrent, much less draw his gun. In a half second he felt a swift shove to both shoulders push him and his groceries backwards, and down the stairs. He tumbled end over end to the bottom, and a second later his intruder jumped over his crumpled body and ran over to Rehnquist's car.

Rehnquist felt himself nearly slip into unconsciousness. He hurt from one end to the other, and couldn't move his right arm. It felt like someone was holding him down. He pulled against whatever was holding him, and through the fog realized that his arm was tangled in the grocery bag, which was now under him and off to his left side. He struggled to free it over the pain of a rapidly building headache, excruciating right shoulder pain, and what surely must be multiple rib fractures. By the time he managed to push himself halfway to a sitting position with his left arm, the intruder had run past him and on toward the street. A few seconds later he heard a car door slam as the car out front sped away.

Chapter Twenty-Seven

Rehnquist freed his right arm from the grocery bag, sat down on the bottom step of the stairs, and tried to clear his aching head. He thought that he could feel an lump expanding on his right forehead, and he gingerly pressed his hand to the spot, to a twitch of pain and the stickiness of blood. Groceries lay all around him, and Hope was nowhere in sight. *How could I be so stupid as to not see this coming?* After a few minutes he was focused enough to slowly stand and began to collect his thoughts. He held the Glock firmly in this right hand, and made his way upstairs.

The house was empty, and as he expected, there were no other intruders. The kitchen cabinets were wide open, and his bedroom dresser drawers had been dumped onto the floor, along with the contents of his closets and his desk. Nothing broken, but a huge mess. It also didn't appear that anything was missing, at least as far as he could tell. Clearly this was not an ordinary burglary, happening just hours after his visit to see Sanchez and Rojas. *Well, I wanted to stir shit up, guess I did.* Ironically, whoever was in his house couldn't have had a clue as to what he was actually looking for, or just how close he was to it, when he was in Rehnquist's car. *Glad I double-locked the trunk and had the keys in my pocket, otherwise the bastard would have had it.*

Rehnquist limped his way back downstairs to collect what was left of his groceries and put them back into the grocery bags, inventorying the damage as he went. Hope was back, sitting at the bottom of the stairs. She was over her fear, and swiftly chewing her way through what was once was a half-pound of sliced turkey breast. Deli meat aside, other than a loaf of bread condensed to a small lump of dough in a ripped bag and enough canned goods for a scratch and dent sale, the grocery loss was minimal. He however, wasn't as lucky; the more he looked, the more scratches and dents he found. *Next time, I'll be more vigilant.* He shook off the pain to his ribs, deciding that they were bruised, not broken, but the hematoma on his forehead was sizeable, and he had a severe bruise to the outside of his right knee.

Rehnquist put his groceries away, applied ice packs to his forehead and knee, and grabbed a beer and sat down at the top of the stairs. As soon as she saw him, Hope ran up the stairs to join him, and for a moment he sat in quiet contemplation while he listened to the excited purring of his four legged friend. After a moment or two he picked up his phone and called Ansco. The call went straight to voicemail. Ansco was good about answering his phone and returning calls, so he must be busy. Rehnquist decided against leaving a second voicemail, and hung up.

Chapter Twenty-Eight

Rehnquist's next phone call was to George. He told him about his uninvited guest, and then explained, "George, I can't get into details right now, but this break-in was the direct result of an unannounced visit that I made today to someone that Jason has been surveilling at the school district."

"Surveilling, how?"

"Electronically, on the district's network. I'm sorry, I can't tell you more right now, you're just going to have to trust me. Grace knows more, and if she wants to tell you, I'll leave that to her. In any case, it will all come out soon. What you do need to know is that Jason playing detective has got him into real trouble, which is why he fled."

"Jesus, you've got to tell me more than that."

"Soon George, day after tomorrow at the latest. I promise. Right now, we have to convince Grace to leave Jason's. Whoever came after me, may pay her a visit too. Can she stay with you and Betty?"

"Of course."

"Okay, let's talk to her. Hang on, and I'll make a three-way."

Once Rehnquist got Grace on the line he quickly told her about the break-in. "Obviously this has to do with my visit to see Sanchez."

"Or Rojas," Grace said.

Rehnquist took a moment to respond. "Or Rojas."

"Nick . . ." George said impatiently.

"Sorry George. Grace, I had to tell George something, so I explained to him that Jason has been surveilling someone at the school district on the district's network, and that that has gotten him into trouble, and that's why he fled. That's all I'm prepared to say right now. If you want to tell him more later that's okay, but right now, we're concerned for your safety. There's a high probability that whoever came after me, may pay you a visit too. So, given the circumstances, you need to leave Jason's indefinitely, and stay with George and Betty."

Grace offered to go home, but Rehnquist didn't think that idea was any better than staying at Jason's, and neither did George. Once they both insisted, she relented. In doing so, she agreed that she *would* feel safer, plus it would be a good chance to catch up—she was long overdue for a visit. Grace and George also agreed that it was time to tell Betty about Jason's disappearance.

After he completed his call, Rehnquist went out and surveyed the damage to his door. The latch had been broken by a screwdriver or other blunt object, and when it still wouldn't give, the frame had been splintered out from around the strike plate. In order to fix it properly, he'd have to replace the lock and at least a portion of the frame. For now, he'd fix the problem by installing a spare hasp and padlock that he had downstairs in a storage unit.

After he secured the lock, he threw his clothes back in their drawers—none too tidy, he just wanted to get them off the floor; he'd straighten them out later. Then he booted his computer and copied Sanchez's emails from the hard drive onto his computer, so that he could finish looking at them later, and then finished by copying all of Jason's journal notes for another, more detailed reading. He would liked to have copied the entire drive; however, his computer's hard drive didn't have enough memory available.

Rehnquist quickly cleaned himself up—at least enough to be semi-presentable in public—then shut down his computer and put it and the hard drive in this backpack. He slung the backpack over his shoulder, locked the door on his way out, and then went down and locked the backpack in his trunk. One quick trip to the bank and post office, then he'd return and start filtering through the rest of the unread emails.

As he was backing out of the drive his phone rang. It was Ansco. "Sorry I missed your call, I was in court."

"Danny, I need to talk to you, but I'd prefer to do it in person. Do you have any time today?"

"Sorry, I don't. I'm due back in court in an hour, and who knows how long I'll be. How about tomorrow? I'm off."

"That'd be fine, I'll drive up. What time?"

"How about noon at Alabama Jack's? That's sort of halfway, and I've been craving their crab cakes."

"Sounds good to me. I'm wide open."

Rehnquist's call waiting beeped. He looked down at the phone and saw that it was Grace. "Danny, I've got another call that I need to take. If I beat you to AJ's I'll grab a table where it's quiet; otherwise, you can grab one."

"Okay, see you tomorrow."

Rehnquist clicked over. Grace was calling to say that she made it to George and Betty's.

"Wow, you made good time," Rehnquist said. "Now I feel better."

"Me too. This thing has gotten so crazy." He could hear the break in her voice. "But I can at least *try* to relax now. Betty went shopping and picked up a few extra bottles of wine, and George says he has beer. You want to stop over for a night cap?"

"I'd love too, but I need to finish up with these emails and map out my strategy for the next couple days."

"Okay, I understand."

"Oh, and Grace, I'm meeting with Ansco tomorrow at lunch. Not sure what I'm going to say, but . . . well, I'll let you know how it comes out."

"Okay.

Nick, before you go, Betty wants to talk to you."

Betty's conversation was short, simple and to the point, an 'I won't take no for an answer' invitation to dinner the next day—fresh fish, and the chance to relax with her, George and Grace. Rehnquist's reply was equally short. "I wouldn't miss it for the world, and I could really use a break. See you tomorrow."

Chapter Twenty-Nine

To get to Alabama Jack's, Rehnquist continued straight onto County Road 905 at the split where US 1 turns toward Lake Surprise and the Jewfish Creek Bridge. The first portion of this trip was none too exciting; roughly ten miles through largely protected natural habitat, which equates to mile after mile of dense tropical hardwood hammocks, and no views of water. When he reached the flasher at the three-way stop, he turned west onto Card Sound Road to continue the remaining five miles or so. This was the part of the trip he liked, because there was always a chance of seeing a crocodile or a bald eagle.

Rehnquist liked bald eagles, but he loved seeing crocodiles. They were modern- day dinosaurs. As a young boy he learned that Florida is the only place in the world where you can find alligators and crocodiles living in the same ecosystem—although not together, since alligators live in fresh water, while crocodiles live in salt water. Rehnquist had seen several alligators in the backcountry lakes of the Everglades fishing with George, but he had never seen one in the Keys. He had heard there were in few on the larger islands of the Lower Keys; maybe one day he'd see one.

He *had* seen a handful of crocodiles—some very close to home. He wouldn't have believed it if he hadn't seen it himself, but once he even saw one swim under the bridge at the Lorelei. Over the past year, crocodile sightings were becoming increasingly common, and you could find them throughout the Keys—often in residential boat canals, much to the dismay of small dog owners. Today, as luck would have it, he saw neither bald eagle nor crocodile. Maybe he'd be luckier on the return trip home.

As he approached the crest of the Card Sound Bridge, he took in a deep breath and took a moment to take in the view. The deep breath brought immediate pain to both sides of his chest, reminding him of yesterday's tumble down the stairs, but it was a picture-perfect day, and it made him feel good just to be alive. At the bottom of the bridge he reached for his wallet and dug for a single to pay the toll. As he approached the toll plaza he slowed and rolled down his window. When he pulled up to the gate, he recognized the toll collector. "Hey Fred, sorry, all I have is a five."

"That's okay, Nick. I thought I recognized the car. Long time no see. How've you been?"

"I'm alright. You?" Rehnquist said, as he turned to hand him the bill. Fred reached for the bill and exchanged four singles. When he looked up from the transaction and saw the side of Rehnquist's face, his eye's widened and his jaw dropped. "Holly shit Nick. What the hell happened to you?"

"I took a tumble down the stairs," Rehnquist said, and smiled. "But I look pretty scary huh?"

"You look like you were in some kind of accident . . . a really bad one."

"I'm fine, thanks. Really. Nothing broken. So how are you?"

"Okay, I guess, but I may soon be unemployed. The Commission is looking at replacing us."

"Replacing you?"

"Automation—Sunpass—they think it's time to modernize."

"Oh. I'm sorry."

Fred nodded and frowned. "Yeah, guess I'll be working at Wal-Mart," he said, then laughed. "Well not really. Whatever happens, I won't be driving to the mainland. I'm three years into DROP, so I may just retire—I'll just loose a year or two of the kitty."

"That wouldn't be so bad, would it?" Rehnquist asked.

"Not for me, I'm ready, but I worry about my buddy Dave," he said, pointing his thumb over his shoulder to the southbound toll collector behind him. He's only got a few years on the job, and he's got a new kid."

"Now that *would* suck. Maybe it won't happen."

"I hope not. In any case, he and the other guys should be okay. The Commission said all nine of us should be eligible for other County jobs, but he'll have a drive—at least to Key Largo—and he lives almost to Kendall."

"There are nine of you?"

"Yep."

"Wow, who knew?"

"Twenty-four seven. You headed to the city?"

"No, just AJ's." Rehnquist glanced into his rearview mirror and saw a car approaching the plaza behind him.

"Well, have a cold one for me, and we'll see you on the way back."

"Okay," Rehnquist said, and waived.

A half minute later he was backing into a parking space on the north side of the road, catty-cornered to the bar.

When it comes to bars, Alabama Jack's is about as unique as they get. It was built in the early '50's, and sits atop a barge, moored among the mangroves. Leaving the Keys, it's just across the county line, a stone's throw from the toll plaza.

Despite the mosquitos and lack of air conditioning, Alabama Jack's is very popular, and therefore, usually crowded. For many Key's tourists, it's their first stop, just before they leave the mainland; for others, it's their last, in the waning hours of their sub-tropical vacation. In addition to the tourists, there's always an odd mix of locals, day-trippers from the city, and even the occasional celebrity, letting his or her hair down and rubbing elbows with the locals. On weekends, the place is usually filled with Miami bikers.

Occasionally a carload of unwitting tourists will see the long line of gleaming Harleys and Gold Wings parked in a perfect row out front, and decide to bypass the place—their collective wisdom the product of one too many '60's or '70's biker movies. Not stopping is a mistake, because these bikers aren't looking for trouble, just a cold beer and a plate of conch fritters. Come Monday they'll all go back to their day jobs: doctors, lawyers, business professionals, cops, and firefighters.

Rehnquist liked Alabama Jack's. He liked the atmosphere, and he like to eat there. Most of the food was nothing special—it was after all, bar food—but in particular, the cooks did wonders with conch: chowder, salad, or fritters; and the sweet potato fries were irresistible. He also liked the unique history of the area.

Card Sound Road was the original, and at one time only road to the Keys, prior to the building of US 1 on the remnants of the railroad bed of Flagler's Florida East Coast Railway following the 1935 Labor Day Hurricane.

At the time of the completion of the Stretch, the north end of Key Largo was mostly undeveloped, and since US 1 was a straighter and more direct route to the populated areas of the island, Card Sound Road was largely abandoned, with the exception of locals who used the area for fishing.

The state owned the road and the land adjacent to it. To accommodate the locals, it sold leases for fishing camps, and a fishing community began to grow on what was then Dade County, just across the county line. Over the decades which followed, squatters erected all manner of structures over the water, many of which were little more than shacks built on barges moored along the waterfront. Rehnquist could still remember coming down to the Keys for the weekend with Julie, and driving past the many eclectic makeshift homes lining the canal which parallels Card Sound Road.

At the time, it reminded him of Houseboat Row in Key West, where a couple dozen houseboats were moored in similar fashion in the waters of the Cow Key Channel, off the east end of the island, adjacent to South Roosevelt Boulevard. The owners had lived there rent-free, and tax-free for who knows how long, and were eventually evicted following years of litigation with the city. The residents of the Card Sound fishing community were similarly evicted by the state, and Miami-Dade and Monroe Counties, only without the litigation and with far less publicity and fanfare.

Rehnquist had mixed emotions about the evictions in both areas. He understood that they were squatters, and the largely lawless fishing camps, in particular, were both a public safety and an environmental disaster; nevertheless, they were also part of the crazy cultural heritage of the Keys and South Florida, and he hated to see them go.

Rehnquist took off his sunglasses so he could see the screen on his phone, and sat in the parking lot for a moment while he texted Ansco to see where he was. He was still twenty minutes out. Rehnquist replied that AJs didn't look busy, so he'd meet him at the bar, then they could move to a table. Rehnquist put back on his sunglasses, went in and sat down at the bar, "Kalik Gold, please," he said, interrupting the bartender's game of 'Candy Crush.'

"Sure, no problem."

Here we go again . . .

Before long Ansco came in and joined Rehnquist at the bar. He ordered a Budweiser and turned to face Rehnquist. "So, what's up?" As Rehnquist began to talk, Ansco saw the bruising. He reached over and pulled off Rehnquist's sunglasses, and set them on the bar. "What the fuck? Nick, what happened to you?"

Rehnquist picked up his sunglasses and put them back on. "I'll explain what happened to me in a minute, but first, you need a little background."

"I'm listening," Ansco said, as he picked up his beer.

"We'd better move over to the table," Rehnquist said, pointing to a plastic patio table in the corner.

Ansco reached for his wallet and plopped it down on the bar. The bartender looked up briefly from her game, and said, "Go ahead, I'll transfer you to Susan."

"Okay, thanks."

Once they sat down at the table Rehnquist began with a little small talk, asking Ansco about his day in court, killing time until the server came to take their order. Once she arrived, Ansco ordered crab cakes with sweet potato fries, Rehnquist ordered conch chowder and conch fritters, and they both ordered another beer.

While they ate, Rehnquist explained about the connection between Sanchez, Grupo Domingo and Rojas; the bid rigging; and how Rojas was heavily involved in drug trafficking, smuggling, and money laundering. When they finished eating, the server collected their plates and brought them another beer without them even asking. Ansco looked impressed. "You know this girl?"

Rehnquist frowned and shrugged. "No, but she must know me."

For the most part, Ansco just let Rehnquist talk, with only the occasional interruption to ask a question for clarity. Once he finished, Ansco sat speechless, eyes locked on Rehnquist. After a moment Ansco picked up his beer and took a long swallow; draining the bottle, never loosing eye contact with Rehnquist. When he finished, he sat his bottle down, and raised his right arm and signaled the server for another round. Finally, he broke the uncomfortable silence. "Okay . . . and how do you know all of this?"

"Sorry, I can't tell you. Not yet—but soon."

Ansco was pissed. "Dammit, what the hell have you gotten yourself into? Obviously this has something to do with Jason, and explains why he's missing."

Rehnquist nodded. "It does, and it's complicated."

"Complicated?"

"Once I sort it out, you'll be my first call."

"Bullshit. So what happened to you and your face?"

"I paid a visit to see Sanchez and Rojas yesterday—"

"You what? Have you lost your fucking mind?!"

"Maybe."

Rehnquist told him about his brief conversation with Sanchez, and that he had received the reception that he expected—and wanted. "Rojas wasn't in his office—not that I expected him to be—but I left my card, with a message to call me."

"Okay, now I *know* you've lost it."

"I just wanted to get their attention. Guess I did," Rehnquist said sheepishly, pointing to his right forehead. Then he told Ansco about arriving home and his unexpected encounter with the intruder. "I feel like such an idiot. How could I have let this happen?"

"I don't know Nick, but it's time to come clean. Totally. You're in over your head."

"Soon Danny, I promise."

"Not soon enough. Are you okay?"

"I'm fine. The canned goods broke my fall."

Ansco grimaced, "Jesus, that sounds painful."

"To be honest, that's the worst part. It'd been so much better if it had only been me. First of all, I wouldn't have had both arms loaded down with shit and I could have shot the fucker. I was as useful as a Secret Service agent holding the First Lady's lap dog. Of all days to choose to fill my pantry. And you know the worst of it? The bastard stole my $36 bottle of Grey Goose out of my front seat."

"Screw the Grey Goose, you're lucky to be alive."

"I know, you're right. I just wished I'd paid more attention to the plates on the black toaster. I never did like those cars; now I like them even less."

When the beers arrived, Rehnquist handed the server his credit card, and said, "I've got this." After she returned with the check and his receipt, he said, I'd better get going, I'm having dinner with Grace, George, and Betty, and I'm supposed to be there in an hour."

"Okay," Ansco said, and extended his hand.

"Thanks for meeting me Danny. I'll be in touch."

"You'd better be. Nick, I mean it—you're up to your ears in shit."

Rehnquist nodded, stood up, and pushed in his chair. "Oh, I forgot to tell you, George and I convinced Grace to stay with him and Betty until this thing blows over."

"Good idea. Hey, before you go, I got the Uber report you asked for. Jason made a request for a pickup at the Marriott by the airport yesterday morning with a drop off at the Federal building downtown . . ."

"Yes?" Rehnquist said impatiently.

"When the driver arrived, Jason was a no show. The driver even went inside the hotel, but no Jason. The desk confirmed he had just checked out, and the concierge was adamant that he didn't want a taxi. He said that Jason told him that he had already contacted Uber."

Rehnquist frowned and shook his head. "So, what's your take?"

"Sorry, no good way to spin this."

Chapter Thirty

Betty opened the door and greeted Rehnquist with open arms. "Come in Nick, and give me a hug."

He stepped through the door and gave her a big hug and a kiss on the check.

Betty stepped back, and held him at arm's length. Now that she had a good look at him she shook her head and was visibly upset. "Oh my goodness Nicky, look at you. Are you sure you're okay?"

"I'm fine Betty," then he paused. "Well, I've had better days, but I've also had much worse."

Betty nodded. She understood.

"Anyway, it's good to see you," he said. "How have you been?"

Betty closed the door and they began walking toward the kitchen. "Fine. Much better now that Grace is here—I was worried about her—but I'm still not over you guys not telling me about Jason."

"Well, that answers that. I guess they told you."

"This morning—finally."

"I'm sorry. That wasn't right, but we didn't want to tell you when we didn't have any answers, didn't know where he was, or if he was alright. For that matter, we still don't know much, but at least I think he's safe." *Or was until yesterday morning,* he couldn't help but think.

"Nick, I'll tell you the same as I told George and Grace. No more secrets. I'm—"

"But—" Rehnquist began to interrupt but was cut short by Betty when she pressed a finger firmly to his lips, stifling him. She gave him a no-nonsense look that he'd never seen from her before.

"I'm a big girl, and don't need to be protected. It's not up to the three of you to decide what I should know, or shouldn't know. Dammit! No more secrets. Got it?"

Rehnquist nodded silently, tail tucked between his legs. He had never heard her curse before, she meant business.

"That said, what a mess he's gotten himself into . . ."

Rehnquist sighed. "He sure has. Hopefully he'll contact Grace soon, or we'll eventually catch up with him. Seems like he's either one step ahead or we're one step behind. When we do find him, we can help him sort things out."

"I hope so," Betty said, her face softening. "Ready for a beer, or would you prefer something else?

"A beer would be great," he said. "Where's George?"

"I sent him to the store, he'll be right back. The lettuce wasn't looking very good."

Rehnquist nodded, "And Grace?"

"She's out back, reading. Why don't you take her a glass of wine? I'm sure she'd appreciate that."

"Sure."

"Grace said you called and that you'd met your detective friend for lunch. How'd that go?"

"As well as can be expected; he's not very happy with me either. But after yesterday, I thought I'd better give somebody in law enforcement a heads up about Jason's troubles—without bringing Jason into it. That's the part he's not happy about."

247

"You mean because he doesn't know the source of your information."

"Exactly."

Betty reached into the refrigerator and pulled out an open bottle of Sauvignon Blanc and set it on the counter, then reached down to the bottom shelf, pulled out an Imperial and handed it to Rehnquist, who was clearly surprised. "George went all out for you."

"Yeah, I guess he did. Thank you."

"So when are you going to tell him the rest?"

"Soon—it'll have to be soon. I just want another day or two to try to find Jason. It'd sound a whole lot better coming from him."

"Yes, it would."

Rehnquist opened the bottle with a Conch Republic bottle opener that was hanging up on the side of the refrigerator, while Betty poured Grace's wine. "Here you go," she said, handing the glass to Rehnquist, "You kids have fun. We'll eat in about an hour."

"Thank you. See you in a bit. Oh, and Betty, I *am* sorry."

* * *

Grace was sitting in an Adirondack chair, under the chikee, reading a thick paperback. When she saw Rehnquist coming, she jumped up for a hug and to take her wine. "Thank you for the wine . . ." she started, and then stopped short. She wasn't prepared for what she saw.

"Thank Betty; I'm just the delivery boy."

Standing there, looking at her, it almost made him nervous. *There's that too good feeling again.* Her hair was pulled back into a ponytail, and she was wearing a white cotton dress and was barefoot, a pair of white flip-flops next to her chair. She was wearing just a touch of makeup, and a delicate fragrance that he couldn't place— not that he knew much about women's cologne these days. "Don't you look pretty?"

Grace's smile broadened, then fell to a frown. "Thank you," she said quietly. "I wish I could say the same. My God Nick, you look awful. I'm so sorry." He had deep bruising under his right eye, which had spilled over to his cheek. The hematoma to his right forehead was still quite prominent, as were the abrasions to his hands, arms and knees. She sat her wine down and gave him a light hug, as if not to hurt him, followed by a tight embrace.

"I'm fine Grace. Really. I promise."

"I don't believe you. You could have been—"

"Please . . ."

Sensing his discomfort, Grace sat back down picked up her wine, and turned to look out at the distant Atlantic horizon. "Gorgeous evening," she said.

Rehnquist sat down in the Adirondack chair beside her and marveled at the simple beauty, light colors giving way to darker hues. "Yes it is." It was a few minutes past seven and the early evening eastern sky was brushed with a thin layer of cirrus clouds, beginning to turn a familiar shade of pink, orange and red. Below it, a band of purplish-gray that would soon grow in size along the entirety of the eastern horizon. The wind had picked up a bit from the light breeze of midday, and small, scattered whitecaps were beginning to form on the water. "I love sunsets on the ocean side."

"I do too," Grace said, as she took a sip of wine. "It's funny, everybody flocks to the bay side to watch the sunset, and they miss seeing how pretty the sky is over here."

Rehnquist nodded in agreement, then sat and quietly stared out at the horizon, wheels turning, in search of a distant childhood memory. After a moment, almost under his breath, he said, "The Belt of Venus."

"I'm sorry, what did you say?"

"The Belt of Venus . . . It's called the Belt of Venus."

"It has a name?" Grace looked bewildered.

"The dark band is the shadow that the Earth casts on the atmosphere, opposite the sunset. The pink band above it is called The Belt of Venous. It's pink because it's lit with backscattered red sunlight."

"I'm impressed. You learned that in school?"

Rehnquist chuckled. "Scouts."

"Really?"

"Yep. If you have a decent Scoutmaster, you can learn some pretty cool things sitting around a campfire. That said, I enjoy watching the sun sink into the water on the bay as much as the next guy."

Grace pondered that thought for a moment, then added, "I used to love watching the sunset down at the Lorelei."

"That's a great spot, but there was one better."

"Papa Joes." Grace said, with no hesitation.

"Papa Joes. Especially those times of the year when it set beside Lignum Vitae Key, over the water, and not behind one of the islands."

Grace nodded and tugged at her ponytail pulled over her right shoulder. "I didn't think you'd lived in the Keys that long."

"I haven't. Julie and I used to come down on long weekends. We'd stay at the Hampton and go to the Lorelei, or eat dinner at Lazy Days, and then go to Papa Joe's, depending upon who was playing where."

"You mean bands?"

"Yeah. Julie loved live music. I miss it—Papa Joes. I was really pissed when they tore it down. Well I guess they had to—before it fell down—so I guess that what I'm really pissed about is that the owners let it get that bad."

"It was such a landmark, everybody loved it," Grace said. "It must have been hard for you; you must have had some emotional attachment to it."

"I did—still do. I can feel it every time I drive by that empty lot. You know, Julie and I had our first Keys snowball fight there."

"Really?"

"It was Christmas Eve and Ginger was behind the bar. She shaved up a pitcher full of ice and we all passed it around. We made snowballs—well, ice balls—and let each other have it."

"That sounds like fun!"

"It was painful. A fistful of ice hits you like a rock. Image the bruises. But it *was* fun—*is* fun, until someone losses an eye," Rehnquist said, smiled, and winked. He took a sip of beer, and then lost in thought, began drumming his fingers on the arm of his chair. After a moment, he suddenly stopped. "So, what exactly did you say to George and Betty about Jason?"

"I didn't tell George anything more than you had already told him. I told Betty about how Jason had suddenly quit work and then disappeared, and how I contacted you—upon George's recommendation—to find him. Then we told her about Jason's extracurricular activities. Boy was she pissed."

"I know. She briefly let me have it when I came in."

They sat in silence for a long moment, just enjoying the evening and the company. Off in the distance in the fading light, you could still make out the white silhouettes of a few gulls against the darkening backdrop of the evening sky. Soon would come the large migrations of pelicans, turkey vultures, and other birds looking to escape the northern cold of winter.

Grace had something that she dearly wanted to ask Rehnquist. A question she had pondered since the morning following their last meeting at Jake's. *He seems relaxed tonight, I'll ask him. If he doesn't want to talk about it, he'll let me know.* She took a sip of courage and turned to gauge his reaction. "Not to pry, but that first night we met, when you said that George was there for you when you needed him more than you could ever have imagined, did you mean when you lost your wife?"

Rehnquist sat expressionless, staring off into the sea. It was nearly a full minute before he spoke. "Julie was adopted when she was five by an older couple who were unable to have children. They were great parents, loved her, and raised her well. They were of modest means, but they managed to get her through college—even her master's program. I met her at a friend's party when she was twenty-five, and I was smitten with her immediately. She had just finished graduate school, and was teaching second grade. I was a year older, had been on the department for about five years, and had just been promoted to detective. By the end of the evening I had asked her out, and after a few dates I was head over heels in love with her. We were married a year later, and settled down to a good life in suburbia.

"Julie lost her mom to breast cancer a couple of years after we were married, and her father a few months later to a heart attack. He was devastated when he lost Julie's mom and he never quite recovered. The way we saw it, he died of a broken heart. I had lost my mother to cancer by the time I was twenty, and like you, my parents were divorced. I was never very close to my father, and had no contact with him after I was twelve. So, since Julie and I were both only children, when I lost her, I lost all the family I had."

Rehnquist took a sip of beer, turned and glanced at Grace, briefly making eye contact, and then looked back toward the water.

"When she was killed, I had her cremated. Hell I didn't know what to do. I thought that's what she might have wanted, but I didn't know—we never talked about it. I hope it was the right choice. Our friends and I had a nice celebration of life for her at her favorite local pub. The next day I brought her ashes down here to the Keys, rented a boat and took them out by myself. I had my own private ceremony and scattered them at the Christ of the Abyss Statue. Afterwards, I took the boat back; drove up to Gilbert's, sat down at the bar and got drunk. I passed out in my car, which is where I spent the night.

"The next day I drove home, and I sat in that house for over a week without a single phone call from anyone. The night of her celebration, all of our friends said things like, 'We're here for you buddy, if you need anything just call.' And there I was, just days after her death, and everyone else had moved on—but me. I thought I was going to lose my fucking mind.

"I had plenty of vacation time at work so I took a month off. I loaded up a suitcase and drove down here, not quite sure what I would do when I got here. I ended up renting a room at the Blue Fin down by the Lorelei, so

I could walk to the bar every day and not have to worry about driving. I paid for a week in advance, although I never planned on checking out—at least not in the conventional sense."

Grace gulped hard. She knew where this was going, and she hated herself for having asked him that night at Jake's 'how have you survived?'

"I started every day with fried eggs and a Bloody Mary, after which I'd spend the rest of the day fishing the pilings off the old Channel Two Bridge. In the evenings I returned to the Lorelei and sat down on the dock back behind the stage and awaited the sunset—not for its beauty, but because it represented my life. After a few more beers to take the edge off, I'd take one for the road, go back to my room, and sit there for the next hour on the edge of the bed with my Glock pressed against my temple, trying to find the courage to pull the trigger and end my pain."

"Oh my God, Nick," Grace said, reaching for his hand. He let her take it in quiet submission.

Rehnquist turned and met Grace's eyes. "I was on an end unit and didn't have anyone next to me. I don't think anyone would have even heard the gunshot. I think the only reason I didn't, was because I couldn't bear the thought of some poor maid walking into my room the next day and finding that mess. I'd seen enough carnage in my life; I sure as hell didn't want to put anyone else through that. Fortunately, that was before the nightmares began."

"Nightmares?"

"Don't ask, that's a subject for another day."

Grace nodded and squeezed his hand.

"Grace, what most people don't understand, is that someone has to clean up the mess. Once the cops complete their investigation and the ME takes the body, they release the crime scene to the owner of the property. There is no magical public employee that comes in to erase the physical stains from the floors, walls, or ceilings. As sad as it sounds, that's left to the family, to either hire a commercial cleaning company or to clean it up themselves, or in the case of a business, it's often relegated to some low-level, underpaid employee."

Just the thought made Grace shiver.

"One evening, toward the end of the week, I was sitting on the dock when a gentleman holding a beer sat down beside me. He didn't look at me, and for the longest time, didn't say a word."

"George," Grace interjected.

Nick nodded. "Back then, at the end of a good or a bad day fishing, George would usually stop by the Lorelei for a cold one on his way home. He had watched me sit there, night after night. On this particular night he decided to join me. He sat there quietly for several minutes, and then finally said, 'Son, you look like you're carrying quite a burden, care to talk about it?' I said, 'No, not really,' and went back to my beer.

"He said, 'OK,' got up and left, and came back a few minutes later with two beers; one for him and one for me. He sat back down and we silently watched the sunset together. Once it had dropped below the horizon, I opened up just a little, and told him that I had recently lost my wife—but I didn't tell him how. He listened attentively, and then we exchanged a little small talk. Then he gave me his condolences, and said, 'I'd best be going. I'll be here again tomorrow night if you want to talk.'

"The next night I was sitting there in the same spot, at the same time, and George walked up with two beers. By the time the night was over I had unloaded and we both had shed a few tears. George suggested that I take a leave of absence from work and stay with him and Betty for a couple of weeks just to sort things out. I thanked him, and told him I'd think about it. When I left, I took the usual beer for the road, but that night in my motel room, the Glock stayed in my bag. George had given me a glimmer of hope.

"Two days later, I met Betty and was staying here at the house. The first two mornings I sat out here under the chickee alone, and watched the sunrise. On the third day George joined me and said, 'I thought that this side of the road might be a little healthier for you. Maybe better to see the sun rise, than to watch it set.' I went fishing with him several times that week. I learned to cast for bait, tie fishing knots, gaff the big ones, and a thing or two about mating a commercial boat.

"After I went back to work I stayed in touch with George and Betty. By now they were a very important part of my life. I tried to keep my shit together at work—I couldn't, you've already heard about that—and when it all fell apart I sold the house, bought the house here on Plantation Key, and moved to the Keys. After a couple of months, I decided that I would do the only thing that I knew how to do, so I got my license and hung up my shingle. I could still be a detective, but hopefully never have to look death in the eye again.

"I'm still not sure why I'm still here—alive that is. Maybe just hoping someday to find the bastard that killed my wife. But what I do know, is that were it not for George, I wouldn't be."

For a moment, Grace let the silence speak for her. Then, she felt compelled to ask, "Did you ever tell George . . . about . . .?"

"The Glock?"

"Yes," she said, softly and nodded.

"Yeah, about a year later."

Grace squeezed Rehnquist's hand. "I'm so glad George was there for you Nick . . . when you needed him most."

"I'm glad he was too," he said.

They sat there for a moment in uneasy silence. "Nick . . . Please forgive me if I'm being inappropriate here. It's not my place to say, but I know you feel responsible for your wife's death—but you shouldn't. It's one thing to grieve for her; it's another to feel responsible. You had no way of knowing what would happen. You have survivor's guilt—the same as survivors from Pearl Harbor or someone who was spared death at 9/11 just because they were late for work."

Rehnquist had had this conversation before, a number of times, and it never ended well. It usually ended in raised voices and hard feelings. Tonight he just listened.

"I have a friend, Karen, who is a flight attendant. One evening when she was scheduled to work, her daughter got sick and she needed to stay home to take care of her. Karen called a flight attendant friend and asked her, if, given the circumstances, she would work for her. Flight attendants can do that—trade shifts. Anyway, her friend traded with her and a few hours later that flight crashed. Karen never got over it, and is haunted to this day. She believes that it should have been her that died . . . that she cheated death. She couldn't have predicted what would happen that night, and neither could you. You shouldn't feel responsible."

"Easier said than done. Have you ever lost anyone really close to you?"

"No, and I can't even begin to imagine what you've been through."

"When you do, that is, when you lose someone that means that much to you, you die with them. Your life loses all meaning and you suddenly have no reason to live—that has been taken from you. If you choose to keep on living, you become a zombie trapped on this side without them. If you choose not to, who knows?"

Rehnquist sat his beer between his legs, took off his sunglasses, and brushed away a tear from each cheek. Then he looked back over his shoulder toward the house. "Well, we better head up."

Grace stood up and took his hand, and on their way upstairs, she asked, "Ever think of reconnecting with your father?"

"No, never. You?"

Grace just shook her head.

Chapter Thirty-One

Dinner was great; a well needed respite from the previous day's trauma, and Betty went all out. Pre-dinner cocktails followed by hors d'oeuvres: sautéed mushrooms in white wine, and shrimp cocktail, served with a nice Sauvignon Blanc, and lots of small talk. Dinner was fresh grilled grouper with black beans and rice, Cuban bread, and a new Malbec that Betty picked up the day before. Dessert was Rehnquist's favorite, Miss Betty's Key Lime pie, double espresso, and while the girls enjoyed after dinner coffee with Kahlua, he and George sipped on white Sambuca, neat, with three coffee beans.

Rehnquist wanted to stay for a night cap, but something told him it was time to go. Time to get a good night's sleep and figure out his next step, now that he had unleashed the wrath of the Miami thugs. He told Betty and Grace goodbye, gave Betty a big hug first, and then, as he hugged Grace, he said "You look tired. Get some rest—Jason's fine. You have to believe that."

"I hope so. Thank you, but right now I'm worried about you." Grace kissed his right cheek, lingering for just a second. "Please be careful. See you tomorrow?"

"Certainly."

Rehnquist met George at the door and they exchanged a pound hug. Rehnquist drew George in close and whispered, "Walk me to my car." They walked out to the landing and began walking down the stairs. "George, I don't want to alarm the girls, but yesterday morning Jason requested an Uber pickup at a hotel in Miami. When the driver arrived, he wasn't there; he had already checked out and left. The driver even went inside looking for him. There may well be a logical explanation for this—maybe as simple as he got tired of waiting and took a cab—but after seeing the shit that he dug up, and after my ordeal yesterday, I'm a little spooked."

"How the hell could you not be?"

"Today I rented a safe deposit box at the Bank of America in Tavernier. In it is the external hard drive you saw at my house. A copy of the entire contents of Jason's computer's hard drive and a trove of archived files are on that drive. Enough evidence to indict at least a dozen people on charges ranging from money laundering, drug trafficking and human smuggling.

"Jesus, Nick."

"I mailed a key to that box to you today. Of course it will go to Miami for sorting before it comes back, so you won't get it for a few days. If anything happens to me, get that key to Danny Ansco. He'll know what to do with it. His phone number is in the envelope with the key.

"Nick, I—"

"I'll tell you more tomorrow, I just don't want to upset the girls. That's why I didn't mention about Jason missing his pickup. I didn't want to tell you, but I had to let you know about the key."

George nodded and looked down at his feet. "I understand. I don't like it, but I understand."

"Okay, I'll talk to you tomorrow," Rehnquist said, climbing into his car.

"Nick . . . please, be careful."

"I will. Thanks George, see you tomorrow."

Chapter Thirty-Two

Rehnquist drove to the end of George's drive and waited for the electric gate to open. It was a marvelous evening, and he had had a wonderful time. Today certainly took the edge off a very stressful week. Tomorrow would be different. Forget what he told Betty about needing another day or two to try and find Jason, it was time to involve the authorities before someone else got hurt. Tomorrow he'd meet up with Ansco and this time, tell him everything—even if it later hurt Jason.

Once the gate opened, as he turned south onto the Old Road to head home, in his headlights he caught a glimpse of someone who was beginning to cross the street stop, turn his way, and waive to him. It was Jeff Riley, George's mate, walking north on the west side of the Old Road. Rehnquist stopped, backed up next to him, and rolled down the passenger side window.

"What's up Jeff?"

"I'm headed up to George's house to see if he can give me a ride."

"Did you call him?"

"No, my phone's almost dead."

"Where're you going?"

"Home, to pick up my truck. My friend Dave is playing over at Marker 88 tonight. I was planning to meet a friend there tonight for dinner, and then hang out and listen to Dave. I've been house-sitting, and since Dave drives right by where I'm staying, he offered to pick me up on his way to work. Anyway, I helped him set up, had dinner, and then Dave asked me to drive down to the Marlin to pick up some cigarettes. Well, his car wouldn't start. The starter just grinds. And of course my other friend had already left—he lives up in Key Largo."

"That sucks."

"Yeah, it does. Dave's gonna leave his car there tonight and have it towed to the shop tomorrow, but he can't leave all of his equipment there, so I'm going back for my truck."

"Hop in, I'll take you."

"Thanks Nick, but it's like, ten miles—the north end of Lower Mat."

"Come on. Besides, George looked pretty tired."

"Well then, I can catch a cab . . ."

"No really, I don't mind."

"You sure?"

"I'm sure."

"Okay, thanks."

The next few minutes, while they drove south, were filled with small talk about fishing and the seasonality of business in the Keys. While they were talking, Rehnquist couldn't help but notice that Jeff was on his phone, texting. *Odd, if his phone is almost dead.*

"Okay, just past the resort on the ocean side. Slow down, you're going to turn left in just a minute. Right here, the next drive."

Rehnquist turned in and pulled down a fairly lengthy drive that was well overgrown by trees and shrubs on both sides. Jeff's old Key's beater Ford was parked off in the turn around. Rehnquist put the car in park and looked over at Jeff. "Well, good luck with Dave and his car."

"He plays for another hour. Care to come in for a beer?"

"I'd like to Jeff, but I've got an early day tomorrow."

"You sure?"

Rehnquist's attention was drawn to headlights in the rearview mirror as a car came down the drive and pulled in behind him. "I'm sure. Besides, looks like you have company."

Jeff opened the door and stepped out, and Rehnquist heard a car door close behind him. The inside rearview mirror was filled with the reflection of the dome light, but in his periphery, in the outside rearview mirror he could see a shadow coming quickly down the drive toward the house. He turned back toward Jeff, who was holding a semi-automatic pistol in his right hand, aimed at him. Rehnquist sat aghast, speechless, just as his door was suddenly yanked open.

Jeff's expression had turned from pleasant and carefree, to quite grave. "No Nick, come on in. I insist." Jeff waived the gun side-to-side for effect. "Now, turn the car off . . . slowly. Leave the keys in the ignition, and get out. And don't even think about trying anything funny. Even if I miss, Manny won't." Pointing toward Rehnquist's back at the rise in his waistband, Jeff said, "Manny, get his gun."

Chapter Thirty-Three

The path beyond the drive was unlit as was the house beyond it, and Rehnquist found it difficult to find his way alongside the overgrown shrubs. The presence of the muzzle of a handgun pressed tightly against his back didn't make the task any easier. Although he only caught a glimpse of Manny when he got out of the car, he looked familiar, and he struggled to recall where he had seen him. Then he remembered. "I recognize you."

"What? Just keep moving."

"I recognize you. You were in my house."

"Shut up and keep walking."

"And you too, Jeff. You were in the car. So what, you're hanging out with two-bit burglars now?"

"I said shut up!" Manny said.

Jeff let out a short, nervous, hyena-like laugh, and walked up alongside Rehnquist, pistol still prominently displayed. "I wouldn't call my friend a burglar, but he is a man of many talents," Jeff said. "Tell 'm Manny. He even drives for Uber—at least Jason thinks he does. Just ask him."

"Jeff, shut the fuck up." The growing impatience was clear in Manny's voice.

"Ask who?"

"Jason, when you see him," Jeff said, followed by another nervous giggle. When they came to the side door, Jeff pulled it open. Manny pressed harder with the pistol, and Jeff said, "Okay, big boy, in you go. Don't worry, we're right behind you."

Rehnquist reluctantly led the way into a dark, sparsely furnished living room, with a couch pushed up against the far wall and end tables on each side. The only light was from two battery operated camping lanterns, one on an end table next to the couch, the other at the end of a dining room table. The house was apparently a foreclosure, with no power, and no AC, and it was stifling. From the looks of things, the previous upside down owners had just walked away, abandoning it.

By now reality had sunk in and Rehnquist expected the worst, but was prepared to fight to the end. How could he have been so foolish as not to have seen this coming? Twice in two days. Keys disease had set in and he'd lost his edge. As his eyes began to adjust to the darkened room, he began to make out a large silhouette at the far side of the dining room. While Jeff held his gun on Rehnquist, Manny walked over to the shadow and handed him Rehnquist's Glock.

The shadow spoke in a thick Latin accent. "Mr. Rehnquist, such a pleasure to meet you. I believe that you have something that belongs to me. Or more precisely, some things."

"I don't know who you are, or what you're talking about."

"I thought that you might have trouble making the connection. Let me help you. Boys . . ."

Manny moved his gun over to his left hand, closed his right fist, and punched Rehnquist below his right ribcage, bringing him to his knees. Jeff followed with a swift blow to the chin, and Rehnquist found himself sprawled out on the floor, with the taste of blood mixed with acid filling his mouth. Manny and Jeff each grabbed an arm and pulled him to his feet. Rehnquist spat blood on the floor and said, "Rojas."

"Ah, see? — cognition returns. Where is it?"

"I still don't know what you're talking about. Where is what?"

Jeff drew back and punched Rehnquist squarely in the abdomen. At first, Rehnquist flailed over, then rallied, stood, and swung wildly at Jeff. Manny kicked the back of Rehnquist's right knee and he went down, just as Jeff kicked him in the crotch. Rehnquist cried out in pain, and then vomited.

"How is your memory now?" Rojas asked.

"I told you . . ."

Rojas kicked him in the side. "Enough. Tie him up, and take his phone. Turn it off and give it to me. He won't be needing it, and we don't need anyone tracking his whereabouts." Manny took Rehnquist's phone and gave it to Rojas.

"I don't have the tape; it's on the boat," Jeff said.

"Useless, fucking useless." Rojas walked over to one of the end tables, grabbed a table lamp and brought it out next to the window. He pulled a knife out of his pants pocket, unfolded it, and cut the cord off the lamp. "Here, use this—on his hands. Don't worry about his feet, we'll get those when we get to the boat. He's going under his own power."

Rojas grabbed Rehnquist's arms and jerked them hard behind him, and then held him with crushing strength while Jeff pulled the lamp cord tight around his wrists. Once his wrists were tied, Rojas spun him around to face him.

"Mr. Rehnquist, I want my files. The data that Roberts took."

"I don't know—"

Rehnquist reply was met with a swift backhand across his face.

"And I don't believe you. You see, the problem is that Roberts wiped his computer and his phone clean, and there's nothing at his house."

His house. Rehnquist stared into the cold darkness of Rojas's eyes, and was suddenly very thankful that Grace was with George and Betty.

"But my sources tell me that you have what I'm looking for."

"Your sources? I found a disk. I turned it over to the FBI."

"Mr. Rehnquist, Mr. Rehnquist," Rojas said, through clenched teeth, followed by another backhanded slap. This one twice as hard. Rehnquist felt a tooth crack.

Rojas picked up his knife and ran it lightly across Rehnquist's throat. When he reached the left side, he made a point of pressing a bit harder. Rehnquist felt his skin give way, and the burn of the warm blade forcing sweat into the fresh open wound.

"I thought that I could convince you to tell me, Mr. Rehnquist, and save us this trouble. But I guess not. So I have another idea. Let's go fishing." Rojas turned to a shadow behind him that seemed to appear out of nowhere. "Frank, get the boat ready, we'll be right there."

Chapter Thirty-Four

Rojas turned his attention back to Rehnquist. "This is your lucky day, Mr. Rehnquist, Mr. Roberts will be joining us." Rehnquist was startled. "Yesterday, he arranged a second meeting with my good friend Special Agent Anders. Anders offered to pick him up, but Mr. Roberts didn't want him to bother. Instead, he insisted that he'd catch a ride with Uber, and meet Anders at his office. Unfortunately, he never made it."

Rojas smiled, and then laughed, obviously pleased with himself. "He really should have taken Anders up on his offer. A lot of bad things can happen to you in the wrong neighborhood in Miami. Once I learned that Mr. Roberts no longer had any records that were unflattering to me or my associates, I thought that all was right with the world. Then you had to come around asking questions. Tsk-tsk."

"Sanchez didn't tell me anything, and I haven't talked to anyone else."

"I'm sorry Mr. Rehnquist, I'm unable to verify that Sanchez didn't tell you anything. You see, he drowned last night in his pool. Looks like he drank too much, passed out, and slipped under the water in the deep end. You know, a heavy tequila drinker really shouldn't swim late at night by himself when his wife is out of town visiting her mother. She will be so sad when she returns home and finds him."

Rojas picked up an old afghan off the chair. "Here, you'll need this," he said, draping it over Rehnquist's arms and shoulders so that it must have looked like a poncho from a distance.

With Manny behind him and Rojas leading the way, they made their way out the back door and onto the pier, which stretched far out over the shallows into deeper water.

"Walk careful Mr. Rehnquist, it's shallow, but I wouldn't want you to fall off into the mud."

The pier was at least a hundred and fifty feet long, and halfway down it Rehnquist realized that he was looking at the stern of Miss Betty. As they approached, Rehnquist said, "That's George's boat."

"So it is," Rojas said. "He loaned it too me, only he just doesn't know it yet. Don't worry, we'll be careful with it. Not that it matters, we won't be bringing it back. We're going to scuttle it when we're done."

When they reached the boat, Rojas stepped up over the gunwale, and onto the deck. "Sorry Mr. Rehnquist, high tide. Boys, please help him up over the gunwale." Manny and Jeff pulled him up and over the gunwale, and onto the deck. He stepped forward with a little encouragement from Manny's pistol, and Rojas stepped behind him. "Goodnight Mr. Rehnquist."

Chapter Thirty-Five

Rehnquist woke slowly, head throbbing, pulsating with every beat of his heart. He hurt in more places than he could begin to count, and any attempt to move or even breathe only added to the pain. Wherever he was, it was pitch dark, and for a moment he remained totally disorientated, unable to remember what happened, or figure out where his was. He could faintly hear the sound of blood rushing in his ears above the whine of wide-open turbocharged diesel engines roaring in the distance. Wherever they were going, they were in a hurry. He fought to concentrate and pull himself out of the fog of confusion, and little by little he began to remember what happened at the house. The last thing he remembered was stepping onto Miss Betty.

Now he was wedged tight into some kind of container. He was on his left side, and as the boat pitched and pounded against heavy seas, a shallow pool of freezing cold water sloshed along his face and side, and the side of his head pounded against something firm and slimy. He was soaking wet and shivering, and the stench was overwhelming. Fish, old fish. His hands were still tied behind him, and he was able to thump the side of the box with his fingers. It was firm and smooth: plastic, fiberglass, or some other composite.

Rehnquist was never prone to claustrophobia, but here he was, pinned tight into a fetal position, legs drawn up tight against his core. And other than the stench, there was almost no air. The space was that small, and becoming smaller with every breath. Now that he was more alert, he realized that he had exhausted most of the air, and would soon pass out from hypoxia. As the space continued to close in around him, he felt himself being pulled down deeper into the darkness, more slime settling against his face. As he began to lapse into unconsciousness, he realized where he was. *Oh my God. Jesus, I'm in a fish box. I'm going to die in a fucking fish box.*

* * *

How long he was out was anyone's guess, but Rehnquist awoke when he began to draw in fresh air. The hatch to the fish box was open, and he could feel someone nudging his bruised ribs. It was Jeff. "Don't die on us. Not yet!" Rehnquist turned toward the sound and was met with a slap to the face. "Okay tough guy, that's all the air you get. We'll be where we're going soon enough." The hatch slammed shut, and Rehnquist could hear the hasp turn, closing it securely.

Several minutes later, the boat still underway, the intensity of Rehnquist's shivering increased as the slimy ice water sloshed around him. The little air that he had received renewed his survival instincts, and as cold as it was, his ability to think. He tugged and pulled at the bonds around his wrists, and could feel them begin to loosen. They had been tied when his wrists were hot, swollen, and bloated, but an hour or so in the icy water changed all that. Now his hands and wrists were cold and constricted, and the water reduced the friction of the wiring insulation against itself and his skin. He could easily wiggle free if he wanted, but it wouldn't help him; he could never get the hatch open. No, he would wait for what he hoped would be a more opportune time. For now, he would maintain the appearance of still being out of it, and tied securely.

He was surprised that his ankles were not bound, and began to pump his leg muscles methodically in an effort to return some blood flow to them. Likewise, he began squeezing his hands into a fist, then releasing them. Maybe, just maybe, he would get at least one chance to save his ass, or at least take out one of them with him. In the meantime, he tried to remember as much about Miss Betty as he could. The layout, features, and where George keep the tools and tackle. This didn't come easy.

He hadn't been out with George in a long time. Too long, but too late to think about that now.

Rehnquist couldn't imagine how long they'd been at sea, but judging by the pounding of the seas, they were well offshore. Some while later—could have been thirty minutes, could have been an hour—he felt the boat begin to slow down and fall off its plane, the engines reduced to near idle speed. Now, the full effect of the seas could be felt, and they began to roll from side to side as they continued to pitch at the crest of every wave. Unsure as to whether it was the seas, the stench of his environment, or his earlier beating, he suddenly felt quite nauseous.

After a moment there was a loud thump on the deck followed by the sound of approaching footsteps. Then he heard the sound of the latch on the fish box being turned and abruptly the hatch was yanked opened. From somewhere in the darkness he heard "Let's go! Time to fish," then Manny and Jeff abruptly pulled him up and out of the fish box by his arms and shoulders, into the light, and onto his feet. At first, his legs began to buckle as he struggled to stand, and it was all he could do to support his own weight. It was also all Jeff could do to contain his excitement. "Dude, you stink like old fish. Tigers and hammerheads gonna love you."

Rehnquist looked up to the bridge where he could see Rojas looking down at him, and the fourth man at the helm. Manny and Jeff walked Rehnquist over to a short bench next to the door of the cabin and they pushed him down onto it. The cabin door was open and the lights were turned up bright, fulling illuminating the deck, gunwales and transom. Having spent that long in the dark, it was too bright for Rehnquist, and it took a moment for his eyes to adjust. He sat back silently as Rojas came down the ladder and faced him.

"He's not going anywhere, but go ahead and tape his legs, just in case—I don't want him flailing around," Rojas said. Jeff went into the cabin and returned with a roll of duct tape. He wrapped three tight turns around Rehnquist's ankles, which pulled mercilessly against his leg hair. Rojas waited until Jeff was finished and said, "Know where we're at Nick? You don't mind if I call you Nick, do you, Nick?" Rehnquist shrugged. "We're out just beyond the hump. You know where that's at, right?"

Rehnquist nodded, expressionless.

"I thought so. Papi used to bring me out here when I was little to fish for sharks. Big sharks . . . You know what we're going to fish for tonight?"

"Snapper?"

Rojas laughed. "Sarcasm. A smart ass to the end. I admire that in a man. A man who knows he's destined for a slow, painful death that's about to begin in just a few minutes, and still he has a sense of humor. We'll see how you do toward the end." Rojas motioned toward the cabin door, and Manny and Jeff went inside. "No Nick, in memory of Papi, we're going to fish for sharks. And guess what we're going to use for bait." A hundred thoughts went through Rehnquist's mind at that point, none of them good, and none contained an ounce of sarcasm.

"Here's the plan Nick," Rojas said, just as Manny and Jeff emerged from the cabin door, dragging a broken, stumbling shadow of a man behind them. Once they reached the brighter lights of the deck, it only took a second for Rehnquist to realize who it was. It was Jason. His arms were behind him, and his legs were taped like Rehnquist's. Rehnquist couldn't see Jason's wrists, but he could only assume that they were taped too. Jason also had duct tape over his mouth. Deep bruises covered his face and upper arms, and it was apparent that he'd been severely beaten. "First we'll start with Jason. We're going to use him for chum—not all at once, but slowly, over time." Jason began to rock back and forth, violently shaking his head.

Rojas smiled from ear-to-ear, as he pointed over to a bait-cutting table extending from an aft starboard rod holder with a fillet knife holstered in its side. "We're going to slowly dismember him . . . a finger here, a finger there, then a toe, maybe an ear, piece by piece into the water. Then we're going to tie a line around him, cut into a few small blood vessels, open up his belly and troll for sharks." Rehnquist looked up and over to Jason. Tears were streaming down his face and he dropped to his knees.

Rojas kneeled down to make eye contact with Rehnquist, and moved to within inches of his face. His stale breath reeked of rum and cigars. For a moment, he stared into Rehnquist's eyes and maintained his smile, and then his chapped lips abruptly flattened and pressed tightly together. Suddenly he looked angry, cold, and cunning. "Then, Mr. Rehnquist, you have a choice to make. You can tell us where the files are, and then we can all wait and have a beer or two while our compadres go pick them up. And once they have them, I'll kill you quickly, then into the water you go. Or, we can slowly cut you up like Jason, and then keelhaul you until you talk, or until the sharks eat their fill. Your choice."

"Boat coming!" Rehnquist heard from the bridge.

"Shit," Rojas said. "Can't be good this time of night. Put them down below, and start fucking with the outriggers. Let's at least look like we're fishing."

Manny and Jeff pulled Jason to his feet, dragged him into the cabin, and then forward, down into the head. Then they returned for Rehnquist. As Rojas started to make his way up the ladder to formulate a plan should they be boarded, he stopped on the third rung, called down to Rehnquist and said, "Oh Nick, should you choose not to talk, when we get back we'll have to see how much Grace knows. And before we do . . . you know, she's a very attractive lady. Perhaps, she'd appreciate a little *special attention*, just to loosen her up." Manny shoved Rehnquist into the cabin and down onto the deck of the saloon, killed the cabin lights and closed the door. Then he and Jeff went for the outriggers, as the boat increased speed.

Chapter Thirty-Six

If there ever would come a time, this was it; the miracle that Rehnquist had hoped for, and he didn't waste any time. The warm, humid air had hastened the blood flow back to his hands, and slipping out of his restraints proved quite difficult, and took much longer than he thought it would. As he struggled to free himself, he could feel the lamp cord cutting into his waterlogged flesh, but after a minute or two, he was finally able to work his hands free. Meanwhile the oncoming boat turned off to their starboard, away from them and toward land. Just as he started for the duct tape he heard Rojas yell, "All clear, let's get started!" from the bridge.

Rehnquist quickly tore the duct tape and scrambled to his feet, just as the door of the cabin opened. Manny never saw what hit him. Rehnquist shoved him hard, back through the door. Manny stepped back once, twice, and before he could recover his footing and balance, a second shove put him over the starboard gunwale into the water. The move was so swift and so sudden that Manny didn't have a chance to let out a peep. The only thing they heard on the bridge was a splash, and when Rojas turned to see what it was, he saw Jeff and Rehnquist grappling around on the deck.

Although adrenaline had kicked in, Rehnquist didn't have much fight left in him. Jeff was lean, light-footed, and half his age; fortunately, he was no fighter, and all he had was flailing hands, and no instinct. If fate had gone his way he would have simply shot Rehnquist, but when the other boat had started coming toward them and Jeff thought they might be boarded, he put his pistol in the bottom tackle drawer, a decision he now regretted.

Rojas looked down in disbelief. "Where's Manny?"

"Overboard!" Jeff yelled up into the darkness.

"Fuck!" Rojas yelled, pulling out his gun. He wanted a clean shot at Rehnquist, and for a second he thought that he had it, just as the captain responded to Jeff's reply. Suddenly the boat slowed and turned hard to starboard, throwing Rojas off balance just as he fired.

Rehnquist heard the blast at the same time that Jeff looked up, startled. Suddenly, Jeff's expressed went blank, as he looked down and grabbed his right upper abdomen, and then fell to the deck. Rojas couldn't believe his luck. "Fuck!" he yelled, firing blindly at Rehnquist as he scrambled for the open cabin door. Not a good choice, but his only choice. He'd be trapped there, but he sure as hell couldn't stay out on the open deck.

By now the boat had reversed course and was heading back for Manny. Rojas looked at the captain. "Can you believe this shit? Go get him."

"I'm running the boat; you go get him."

Rojas pressed the hot muzzle of his gun tight up against the captain's right temple. "Frank, I said go get him. I can run the boat; it's not fucking rocket science. And get shithead's gun too."

"Watch out for Manny."

"No shit, Dick Tracy," Rojas answered, through clinched teeth.

Frank reluctantly left the wheel and started down the ladder. Under his breath he mumbled, "I don't get paid for this shit."

Chapter Thirty-Seven

Seconds quickly ticking by, Rehnquist fumbled blindly in the dark, frantically searching for anything that he could use as a weapon. Nothing. Not even a real fork, just a goddamn box of plastic ware and paper cups. This was a fishing boat, all right—all business—and all the sharp stuff was secured somewhere out on the deck. Not even a fucking bottle opener. *Damn twist-offs, why can't George drink real beer?*

Rehnquist was standing in the doorway of the cabin when Frank started down the ladder. He was expecting Rojas, but was surprised to see that the feet were attached to much smaller silhouette—the captain—who cautiously lumbered down the ladder, gun in his right hand. When he was four rungs down, Rehnquist quickly stepped back into the darkness of the cabin, where he could see, but hopefully not be seen; surprise being his only option.

Rehnquist stepped to starboard—his left—just inside the cabin door. As he pressed up tight against the wall, he bumped up against something he had previously missed, bringing a smile to his face. He recalled having used one like it several years before to subdue a neighbor's out of control Pitbull that was loose and on the attack, back when he lived in the city. This could be the answer to his prayers.

Frank hesitated at the base of the ladder, trying his best to see. Jeff was laying, moaning, on the deck next to the starboard side of the transom, and his gun was nowhere in sight. The cabin door was open, and in the moonlight Frank could see all the way to the forward saloon wall, but the area forward of that, going down toward the head and v-berth, was pitch dark. Frank cautiously took a step toward the cabin and reached through the door and off to the side for the cabin light switch.

Rehnquist was ready. He extended the tip of the fire extinguisher out into the door opening and squeezed the handle. Two pounds of dry chemical fire retardant greeted Frank right square in the face. He screamed and fired blindly three times into the darkness and grabbed his eyes. He couldn't see anything, but whatever it was came from the starboard side, so he fired two rounds into the wall. Rehnquist rolled to port, exposing himself for a half second through the open cabin door, as the final two rounds trailed behind him.

Once the magazine was empty and he heard the slide stop engage, Frank knew that he was fucked. Rehnquist also heard it, and came out swinging the light fire extinguisher, striking Frank sharply on the left side of his head. He staggered, fell back against the ladder, and dropped to the deck unconscious. Rehnquist picked up the fire extinguisher and kicked Frank's gun back into the cabin, and then retreated back to his original position, just inside the door.

As long as the shots were firing, Rojas wasn't going anywhere. But after hearing the heavy thud against the ladder—followed by silence—he had to look. He left the wheel and carefully leaned over the bridge deck. There, in between the ladder and the cabin door, lay Frank, face down on the deck, and no sign of Rehnquist, or Frank's gun. *In-fucking-credible. What's so hard about this? This should have been easy. Who is this fucking guy? — James Bond? —MacGyver? And what's with the help? Of all the people I could have brought, I brought the Three Fucking Stooges. So much for honoring Papi's memory.*

Totally distracted by the situation at hand, Rojas almost forgot that they were underway. When he remembered, he stood up and quickly scanned the horizon for lights, corrected course, and then increased speed as the boat was beginning to yaw in the following sea. One last scan for lights, then he headed down to complete the job himself.

Rojas had lost count of how many rounds were fired, but he was sure of one thing, most likely Rehnquist was in possession of someone's gun. He had no choice but to go down the ladder, and he figured his best odds were to scurry partway down, pistol in hand, and then drop the remaining distance to the deck. He didn't want go too slow, as he was expecting to see a muzzle flash. Just as he stepped down onto the second rung, he heard something thump hard against the bow, followed by a momentary loss of RPMs in the port engine. "Manny," he said aloud, and shrugged.

Rehnquist was as ready as he could be with the empty two-pound fire extinguisher, and the second Rojas hit the deck, Rehnquist stepped out from the cabin and catapulted the canister toward him. Rojas threw up both arms simultaneously and deflected the blow; however, the force of the impact and his quick reaction caused him to become unbalanced and topple over backwards. When he fell, the pistol flew from his hand and onto the deck, and slid almost to the transom, with the fire extinguisher coming to rest beside it.

Unfazed by the fall, Rojas immediately rolled over onto his hands and knees, and as he scrambled to retrieve the gun, Rehnquist quickly weighed his options. Going for the gun was out of the question; he was too far away. So was the prospect of pummeling Rojas before he could reach it. Rojas had him by at least fifty pounds, and the memory of his earlier death grip on his arms gave

Rehnquist good reason to keep his neck a safe distance away from those mammoth hands.

No longer in possession of the fire extinguisher, Rehnquist's only hope was to find another weapon. Rojas was between him and his obvious choice, the fillet knife on the bait-cutting board, so he had to find something else—quickly, and out on the open deck. There was no point in going back down below. There was nothing down there, except Frank's empty gun, and he and Jason would be sitting ducks. In desperation, and hoping against all hope, Rehnquist quickly looked from side to side—nothing.

With no one at the helm to hold the rudder or to adjust to an appropriate speed, Miss Betty began to languish, pitching and yawing in the following sea. Suddenly, the stern pitched high into the crest of a single large wave, pushing the bow down, and causing her to heel to port, and then broach to starboard.

The unanticipated motion threw Rojas over and onto his right side, but Rehnquist managed to right himself—thereby averting a fall—by quickly stepping down into the heel, and grabbing onto the starboard rail of the ladder, just before Miss Betty turned broadside. As soon as the wave passed, she settled into its trough and began to take moderate seas abeam, rolling first to starboard, and then to port. Rehnquist held on for the roll to starboard, and then, as he leaned back away from the roll to port, he saw it—the glint of moonlight on metal.

Stowed in a horizontal rod holder on the port side was a long, wide-throated gaff, the kind used for landing large, powerful fish. Rehnquist grabbed it a split second before Rojas reached the gun, and was mid-swing when Rojas rolled over, sat up, and pulled the trigger.

Rehnquist heard and saw the muzzle blast and felt his right leg buckle beneath him, immediately followed by a dull burning pain in his right thigh, and the sound of Rojas screaming in pain. The top loop of the gaff had made contact, deflecting Rojas's aim, knocking the gun out of his hand, and shattering his right wrist.

Rehnquist steadied himself against the roll of the seas and rose to his feet—bringing the gaff up with him. Rojas was lying on his right side, curled over, holding his wrist. When he saw Rehnquist get up, he quickly looked to his right and saw the gun—just out of reach.

Rojas looked up to Rehnquist, and then back to the gun. "You're dead, motherfucker."

"I don't think so," Rehnquist answered, and took another swing.

Rojas rolled quickly to his left, and the hook missed his head by little more than an inch. Before Rehnquist could draw back for another swing, Rojas slammed his right foot down onto the gaff, knocking it from Rehnquist's hands. Rojas then rolled over, pinning the gaff to the deck with his right thigh while he reached for the gun.

For a moment, Rehnquist struggled to lift the gaff from under the strain of Rojas's weight, until Rojas came up short in his reach, and rose up on his knees to shorten the distance. When he did, Rehnquist picked up the gaff, turned the hook horizontal toward Rojas, and swung it waist high, with the intention of grabbing Rojas around the neck and pulling him backwards—the Vaudeville Hook—time to pull the bad actor from the stage.

By the time Rojas realized his dilemma, it was too late. Just when the open throat of the hook came around his neck, he lunged left, and forward. Rehnquist pulled back hard with both hands. He heard a muffled gasp and felt the tip of the hook connect with thin muscle, gristle, and bone. Rojas collapsed, and when he did, Rehnquist went with him, unprepared to receive Rojas's deadweight.

When Rehnquist fell, the gaff handle was pulled from his hands and onto the deck. Rojas's lifeless body lie before him, his head turned hard to the left, the business end of the gaff extending through the back of his neck.

Rehnquist struggled to his feet, dragging his injured leg behind him, and made his way over to the body for closer inspection. Rojas blinked. He still had a pulse, but not for long. He was conscious, but paralyzed and breathless. Unconsciousness would come within seconds, and soon after, his final heartbeat. Rehnquist looked into his eyes. They were vacant, and for a second, he imagined that he could see through to his soul. Rehnquist didn't say a word. He waited a few seconds for the final blink and then just long enough to ensure that he was the last thing that Rojas saw before he met his maker.

Rehnquist picked up Rojas's gun, slipped it into his waistband, and climbed up to the helm. He put both engines in neutral and turned on the NAV lights, looked at the chart, and noted their coordinates. Then he set a waypoint on the chartplotter so that later the Coast Guard would have some record of their location when they came looking for what might be left of Manny. Rehnquist's phone and someone else's was on the console, but it didn't matter, they were too far out for cell service—probably too far out for VHF. By now, they were out in the shipping lanes—or beyond. Maybe after he set Jason free, he could hail a ship and have them relay a message to the Coast Guard on Single Sideband.

Rehnquist went back down to the main deck to check on Jeff. He was semi-conscious, holding his hand over the gunshot wound. There was very little blood on the deck, but his abdomen was severely distended from internal bleeding. "Why'd you do it, Jeff? Were you a plant, or did they recruit you after you started working for George."

"Help me," he moaned.

"Son, there's not much I can do for you. Looks of that wound, he took out your liver. This far out, you're not likely to live long enough to make it to shore. Sorry, you should have stuck with mating boats." Rehnquist quickly checked Jeff's his pockets and waistband for guns or other weapons, then went back to Frank who was just beginning to stir. Rehnquist didn't want to kill him, but he needed to put him somewhere safe, on ice for a little while. He knew just the place.

Once Frank was no longer a concern, Rehnquist stepped into the cabin, turned on the lights, and went forward, down to the head. He opened the door to a visibly shaken Jason, trembling in fear. "It's okay, you're safe now." Rehnquist bent over and pulled Jason forward, tearing at the duct tape wrapped around his wrists, which had obviously been on a long time. His hands were a mess, all purple and swollen. When he finished with his wrists, he started on his ankles. "I'll leave the one on your mouth to you, that's gonna hurt."

Jason started to pull the tape away slowly, but gave it a quick pull instead, bringing with it a couple of layers of skin and several days of stubble. Still trembling, he looked at Rehnquist and stammered, "Wh-who are you?"

Rehnquist steadied his injured leg and slipped his arm around Jason. Anchoring his hand around his right shoulder, he began to pull him upwards, and to his feet.

My name is Dominic Rehnquist.   Grace sent me—she's worried about you.   Now come on, let's get you home."

Epilogue

"Shrimp please," Rehnquist said, as he picked off the decapitated shrimp head from the jig.

George looked up in disbelief. "You're not supposed to feed the fish; you're supposed to catch the fish. Maybe you're not hooking them right."

Rehnquist let out a few extra feet of line and dropped it down to George. "Okay big fisher guy, you do it, show me how." Rehnquist had been standing atop the poling platform on George's skiff for the better part of an hour, casting to a small patch of dense seagrass in the otherwise sandy flat.

"There you go, that should do it. That shrimp's going nowhere. Guaranteed to bring in a fish." Rehnquist nodded a thank you, then cast toward the grass. The lightweight line seemed to hover for a second before landing almost dead center in the patch, close to where he had seen the last shimmer. *Perfect*. He jigged the tip of the rod ever so slightly, and then watched his line twitch one, twice, and then he felt a tug. He responded by pulling back sharply on his rod and felt the line go slack. He reeled in for another cast with a clean, shiny hook.

"Shrimp please."

"Geez Nick, are you kidding?"

"Sorry, this one's aggressive—and smart. Pretty soon I'm going in after him with my hands."

George brought him a cold beer and two shrimp. Rehnquist picked up his empty beer bottle, pulled it out of the koozie, and swapped it for the cold one. He handed the empty down to George and took a long swallow. "What's with two shrimp?"

"Thought I'd save myself a trip."

George picked up his rod and went up to the bow, working a small ledge off to starboard. They were anchored up in a few feet of water over a beautiful sandy bottom at Cape Sable, near the tip of Middle Cape. Grace and Jason were frolicking on the beach, chasing each other around like two little kids. It was a beautiful day, mid-eighties with a light breeze under a cloudless sky.

"Four more indictments yesterday," Rehnquist said. "Did you see the Herald?"

"No, I don't read those damn Miami newspapers, nothing but bad news."

"Sorry, old habit. I saw it on the online version this morning. Two foremen, a tax accountant, and another cop."

"Foremen? Already going after the little guys?"

"Looks like they were involved in the cash wage payments. Colombian and a Mexican—must've thought they were a flight risk. That, and they probably assume they'll be willing to rollover on some higher-ups in exchange for a deal." Rehnquist finished threading another shrimp onto his jig. "Wow, these shrimp are huge, we should be eating them."

"Help yourself."

"You know I could never understand why the shrimp we buy to eat are way more expensive and often smaller than the ones we buy at the bait shop for next to nothing—and they're still alive."

"All about the water they're raised in."

"Oh sure, like the ones at the Fisheries were raised in the gardens at the Ritz."

"Looks like you've got a bite," George said, pointing toward the bobbing line. Rehnquist pulled back on the line and it went limp, just as a pelican crashed down in the water beside them. "George looked at the pelican then up to Rehnquist as he was reaching down to pick up the second shrimp. "The pelican must have heard you're giving away free shrimp."

"Very funny," Rehnquist said.

"The arrests? How big's this thing?"

"Huge. Bigger than Jason could have imagined. And Ansco told me his FBI guy says it probably involves at least three other school systems as well."

George whistled, "Sounds like somebody has their work cut out for them."

Rehnquist laughed. "Somebody? Lots of somebodies. FBI, DEA, ICE, TSA, FDLE, PD, SO, and every other goddamn acronym you can think of. Oh, forgot one. After our little adventure on the high seas even the USCG. Everybody wants a piece of this one. Hell, they're still trying to sort out who has jurisdiction." Glad I'm done with my part."

"So who's leading the investigation?"

"Good question. Right now, publicly they're running things as a task force, but I can only imagine what it's like when they're behind closed doors."

The breeze had picked up slightly, and when Rehnquist cast his line, it fell several feet short of the grass patch. He reeled it back in, and this time put his back into it. He watched in bemused horror as his line went one way, and the shrimp another. Fortunately, George was busy watching the activity on the beach. Rehnquist turned his head back in time to watch the pelican gobble his shrimp. He decided to just leave the line in the water. What George didn't know wouldn't hurt him. Besides, he couldn't do any worse with just the rubber jig.

George reeled in his line, checked his bait, and recast. "Do you think Jason will stay out of trouble?"

"Without a doubt, I'm sure of it. Of course, someday he and I will be asked to testify about our involvement, but it will be from the victim's side, and they'll downplay the data breach. I talked to the assistant state's attorney on this, who is an old friend of mine from the city—another cop turned lawyer. He said the state wants no part of a prosecution, and neither do the Feds. The fact that this had been going on for so long is a huge embarrassment for all the agencies with oversight and enforcement, so they'd like to keep Jason's role as quiet as possible. Regardless of how he obtained his data, and however illegal it may have been, no one cares. The forensic accountants are having a field day. They can't use any of his data as evidence of course, because of the way that it was obtained, but it became a compass needle for everything that they found. He'll end up making them all look good, so he's safe."

"Good, I worry about him."

Rehnquist became bored with the show, and as he reeled in his line for the last time, said, "Enough of this shit. I haven't caught anything all day." Just as the end of the line reached the boat, an osprey dove down to within a few feet of the spot where he had last felt a tug on his line, and seized a mangrove snapper. The osprey then flew almost eyelevel to Rehnquist several yards off the stern, and landed on a large piece of driftwood at the edge of the shoreline, where it quickly began to devour its meal.

George howled with laughter. "That's how it's done Nick; now tell me God doesn't have a sense of humor."

Rehnquist sat down on the poling platform and began to pay attention to the rest of the world, the world beyond that small patch of grass.

"I've been thinking about selling the big boat, George said."

"Miss Betty? Why would you do that?"

"I don't know; I've been thinking about it for quite a while. Some days I think I'm getting too old to run her anymore. It's too much work."

"Cut back, just run when you want to."

"That would be fine, but it's awfully hard to keep a mate that way."

"Hope the next one's better that the last one."

"My bad, should have run a background check. Guess I'm too trusting."

"Wouldn't have helped with the captain. Frank's record was clean as a whistle. How about the other guys that freelance?"

"That's such a mixed bag. Some of them are alright, but most aren't worth a shit, which is probably why they're freelancing. I don't know, I may just go back to running the occasional backcountry charter."

"Sounds like a plan George, but are you really ready to sell the old girl?"

"Maybe, but it'll be a while, I've got some bullet holes to patch that have adversely affected the resell value."

"Don't go blaming those on me."

"Well if you hadn't been so damned slow, maybe you could've taken out the bad guys before they did so much damage."

"Thanks, George. Maybe you should just leave those holes . . . hell of a conversation piece."

"Yeah, and if that's not enough, there's always the languishing memory of the three ghosts."

"True, that's enough to give a potential buyer pause.

George pointed over to Grace and Jason, still horsing around on the beach. "'bout time to join them and see what Miss Betty has prepared for us in today's picnic basket."

"Yep, but I'm sure enjoying watching them."

"Jason looks happier than I've ever seen him," George said.

"He does look happy." *Something about cheating death tends to put a certain stride in your step.*

George looked at Rehnquist; Rehnquist could almost read his thoughts. His eyes reddened, and he started to tear up. "Nick, I can never thank you enough—"

"Stop. We've been through this before."

"I know, but—"

"No buts, just give me another beer, that's thanks enough. Besides, if you hadn't been there for me, I couldn't have been there for you.

George nodded, and then reached in the cooler and handed him a fresh one. Rehnquist pulled out the empty and handed it to George, then stuffed the cold one in his koozie. George dropped the empty into the recycling bucket and grabbed a cold one for himself. They toasted the day, good times spent together, and the happy 'kids' on the beach, walking arm in arm, laughing at God knows what.

The boat rocked gently in the water, and the cool breeze blew through their hair, the sounds of seagulls and terns all around them. Off in the distance was a flock of white pelican, and Rehnquist saw his first Roseate Spoonbill in years. He pointed to it and George said, "Don't see them very often anymore. Glad there are still a few left. They just don't seem to migrate back here like they used to."

"Too many people George, we fucked it all up."

George nodded in agreement. "You can't believe the changes I've seen since I was a kid."

"No, I can't, but I've got a pretty good idea. Still, it doesn't get much better."

Rehnquist jumped down from his seat on the poling platform, handed his beer to George, and walked forward and began to pull in the anchor line, bringing them closer to the beach, and out of the now waist deep water. Grace saw them and waived. "We'll be over in a minute," Rehnquist hollered to her.

"She's pretty Nick."

"Yep."

"And she's nice."

"Yes she is, and your point?"

"No point, I'm just saying."

Rehnquist pulled in enough line that bow lightly touched bottom, then continued to pull until he'd beached the boat a foot or two. Then he tied off the line, and reached for his beer from George. "Thought I was too old for her?"

George held out Rehnquist's beer to him and said, "You're not suggesting, that I'm suggesting . . .?"

"Heavens no, George. Here, help me with the cooler." They each grabbed one end and set it up on the gunwale.

Not quite ready to admit defeat, George said, "And not to sound like an old pervert, but you have to admit that she looks pretty good in that white bikini." Rehnquist looked up, as if he hadn't noticed. Jason was lying in the sand making a sand angel, and Grace was standing over him laughing.

Rehnquist climbed down off the boat, and George followed. They grabbed the cooler and pulled it down off the boat, and began walking toward the beach. Rehnquist stopped for a second and said, "George . . . I'm not looking for romance."

Grace saw them coming in from the water, and leaving Jason behind, began walking their way. "Maybe not Nicky, but maybe romance is looking for you."

GARY E. BOSWELL

ABOUT THE AUTHOR

Gary and Marcia Boswell are originally from Central Indiana, and have been married since 1981. In 1983, Marcia gave birth to their forever pride and joy, Ian Merritt, and for the next several years, the three of them and Ian's kitty Mercedes lived in blissful ignorance of what life had to offer at the 25th parallel.

In 1988, the Boswells made their first visit to the Florida Keys to visit Marcia's brother Mark. Like so many visitors before them, that first vacation turned into a second, the second turned into a third, and for the next several years, the Keys remained their annual pilgrimage. In 1996, they said goodbye to Indiana, and the Keys became home.

Printed in Great Britain
by Amazon